STAR WARS™

JOIN THE RESISTANCE

ATTACK ON STARKILLER BASE

STAR WARS

JOIN THE RESISTANCE

ATTACK ON STARKILLER BASE

WRITTEN BY

BEN ACKER & BEN BLACKER

ILLUSTRATED BY

ANNIE WU

DISNEY
LUCASFILM
PRESS

LOS ANGELES · NEW YORK

Acker and Blacker want to dedicate
this book to everyone who resists.

CHAPTER
01

MATTIS BANZ FOUGHT hard to stay focused on what was happening. The struggle to pay attention was a war he would never stop fighting, no matter how many battles he lost along the way. At that moment, maintaining focus shouldn't have been a problem. Mattis and J-Squadron shot through space in a Hutt's ship to save their squad mate Jo Jerjerrod from the First Order. It should have been easy to concentrate, but it wasn't. Mattis's mind wandered, as it always seemed to. It wandered, then broke into a run, and then leaped about as if his recent memories were puddles in which to splash around.

He sprinted through his recollections of leaving his homeworld, Durkteel, joining the Resistance, screwing up, getting in trouble, and being sent to collect scraps with the rest of J-Squadron on the swamp planet Vodran. There Mattis had been caught by the First Order, locked up by a detestable officer named Wanten, and convinced that his friends had died or been reprogrammed and that he was going mad. He *hadn't* gone mad. His friend AG-90 hadn't been reprogrammed. His friends were—with the exception of poor excitable Klimo, who had been eaten by rancors—still alive. Despair had given way to hope. They'd broken free from captivity, crawled through the swamp, and battled squads of stormtroopers before escaping the planet. Wanten had kidnapped Jo in the process, but they were hot on his trail. Still, there was one puddle in which Mattis kept splashing. One memory that distracted him from focusing on the current race through space: *Lorica had used a lightsaber!*

Lorica Demaris, his Zeltron squad mate, was the toughest, smartest, coolest person Mattis had ever met. And Mattis had grown up on stories of the Jedi, an ancient order of the toughest, smartest, coolest members of the galaxy. Seeing Lorica wield a lightsaber, the weapon of the Jedi, created an irresistible mental puddle for Mattis. He could jump and slosh around and kick the water of it for days, even weeks. Jedi connected with the Force, the ancient source of power that flowed through every living thing. Mattis knew that one day he would be a Jedi. He had the Force flowing through him, even though the Force didn't seem to know it yet. Someday the Force would be his, and Lorica's, too, and they would have their own lightsabers, and they would be Jedi Knights. For now, the excitement of Lorica's natural ability with the lightsaber was a taste of what Mattis was certain would come for them. It thrilled and understandably distracted him.

His state of distraction wasn't helped by Lorica's pacing the boxy ship like a caged tawd. He watched her and could tell she was a coiled spring, eager to *do* something. The mud of their escape that caked her—all of them—had dried and was flaking off with every step. She barely seemed to notice it. Mattis didn't blame her for her restlessness. She was closer to Jo than any of the rest of them were; she wanted him back with a stronger fervor. Mattis weighed whether or not to interrupt Lorica's pacing. On the one hand, maybe he could distract both of them from their helplessness with a conversation about what he desperately wanted to talk about: the Force. On the other hand, he couldn't contain himself anyway.

"*You fought with a lightsaber,*" Mattis burst out.

Lorica let out the kind of long breath she had come to exhale whenever Mattis told her something about herself she already knew.

"Those stormtroopers didn't stand a chance!" Mattis continued. "You sliced a speeder bike down the middle! You said you're not a Jedi, but you also said there's no such thing, which is wrong, so maybe you are one after all! What I want you to do is think about, really consider, whether or not you felt something when you used that lightsaber."

"It was great. The heft was perfect. It felt right in my hand. I felt something, sure." Lorica shrugged.

"The heft?"

"The weight of the thing in my hand."

"I know what *heft* means," Mattis said, screwing up his face in expectation of more. "But . . . that's all you felt?"

Lorica seemed to weigh the heft of this question as she had that of the weapon back on Vodran. "After being locked up in a cell for so long," she finally said, a bit more quietly than before, "it felt good to let loose. It felt good to, I don't know, act a bit crazy, you know?"

After his experience in the First Order prison on Vodran, Mattis preferred not to talk about craziness. So he said, "Slicing a speeder in half isn't, like, an easy thing to do. I'm pretty sure."

Lorica's face split into a wide smile. "It was pretty amazing, wasn't it?" she said, a throaty glee coming into her voice. "Just two halves—thunk, thunk—crashing into the mud."

"But what did it *feel* like?" Mattis pressed.

"Good."

"No."

"Yes," Lorica corrected him. "Good."

"And?"

"Violent?"

Mattis twitched in frustration. From her expression, he could tell that not only was he not getting through to Lorica—he wanted her to tell him that she felt something spiritual move when she wielded the lightsaber—but she was getting annoyed with him for pestering her when, clearly, her mind was elsewhere.

"I don't know what to tell you, Mattis," she said, the corners of her lips turning down in a frown. "Good and violent. That's how it felt. If those feelings are the Force, then I guess I'm a Jedi. Someone call Yoda."

"Hey!" Mattis barked in a voice squeakier than he'd intended. "I told you stories about Yoda because I thought you'd think they were cool!"

This made her smile. "I'm just telling you that I think those feelings are just feelings, not some dusty old grandpa religion." She shrugged again matter-of-factly. "I'm Zeltron," she said. "We know about feelings."

He remembered how, back on Vodran, Lorica had magnified the emotions flying around. She'd intensified his feelings and those of their captor, Ingo Salik. Perhaps she'd magnified her own.

Mattis couldn't tell what had been intentional. He wasn't sure he wanted to know. Feelings were often confusing. The Force was something he could hold on to.

So he told her, "The Force is a great cosmic power but also so quiet that unless you're looking for it, you might mistake it for regular feelings and miss it."

He explained that even if you hunted for it within yourself, as Mattis had his whole life, you might still miss it somehow. That was how potentially subtle the Force could be. It might just take time to emerge. He told Lorica that the Force had many facets. It could make a warrior great with a lightsaber or it could make a chef versatile with a recipe. It focused what was inside you. It could warm you when you were cold.

"It can make you taller or faster or able to speak any language. It can let you talk to colors and ask them questions. Some people can fly using the Force, but the best thing about it is that it connects you to everyone and everything in this deep web of understanding. It's like being hugged but from the inside. It can be hard at first, but don't worry. I'll teach you how to use it, because it's time I told you," he said. "It's time I told everyone." Mattis avoided eye contact with the group. He raised his voice and admitted, "I have the Force. It's inside me. It hasn't come out yet, but it's in there." He let that land and then quietly asked Lorica, "What better way to draw it out than to train you in its ways?"

Mattis felt brave for having finally admitted to everyone once and for all that he had the Force. He had implied it before and even confided in some of them. But this was his first time admitting it outright to everyone all at once. Lorica made him feel brave. He looked around at his friends to see how they were taking his news and how they regarded his bravery. Lorica had gone back to pacing. She was probably processing his offer. She hadn't had anything to learn from Mattis so far—she was usually the one who did the teaching—so the idea of learning from him must have felt new to her. AG-90 was busy flying the ship and, as a droid, probably needed to focus on that and would think about Mattis later. Ymmoss the Gigoran was copiloting and so was probably similarly busy. Dec and Sari were glued to the viewport in awe of what had just appeared on the other side.

"How'd you do it, Brother?" Dec asked AG. "How'd you find them out here in all this empty space, them with a head start on us, us with no way to track them and no idea which way they were heading?" He pointed to Wanten's ship out in the meteor field ahead of them, with Jo aboard.

"Jedi space magic. I'm a Jedi. I never told you? I Jedi'd it. It was easy," AG-90 said, evading the meteors bent on colliding with their ship. Mattis knew that AG's teasing was just his way of dealing with the enormous disruptor bomb of a revelation he had exploded on them. It would take them some time to accept it. He'd be there for them once they reckoned with this new information about him. He was their friend. Besides, being there for his friends was what a Jedi would do.

CHAPTER

02

DEC HANSEN was leaning over his brother's piloting station, his eyes flicking among the console, the viewport ahead, and AG's copilot—the thick-bodied, woolly Gigoran called Ymmoss. Dec liked Ymmoss as much as he could like someone he'd just met, which in Dec's case was a lot. Sure, he hadn't liked Jo Jerjerrod when they'd first met, but that was different. Circumstances were complicated, what with Jo being Dec's commanding officer and Dec having very little interest in being commanded. But he liked Jo just fine now. After all, they were chasing a First Order ship to try to rescue Jo, weren't they? And they were giving good chase, thanks to AG.

"I mean, really good flying, Brother," Dec told AG again.

Dec shot a glance at Sari, who was maintaining the information console but watching him out of the corner of her eye. Dec knew that *she* knew that he was trying to insert himself into the entire piloting affair, rather than just standing back and letting the others take control.

"I bet the reason they say droids shouldn't be pilots is because we're too good at it; we'd put everyone else out of a job." AG chuckled to himself as he closed some distance between their ship and Wanten's.

His droid brother didn't seem to be getting the drift of Dec's point, so Dec added, "Imagine what-all you could do with kin sitting next to you." He smiled at the furry white copilot.

Ymmoss would not relinquish the seat no matter how many ways Dec offered to relieve her. AG and Dec had been raised together as brothers on Ques, where kin was thicker than water, no matter how thick the marsh. It should be Dec flying copilot for his brother, regardless of how much Dec liked this woolly interloper.

AG-90 never took his ocular sensors off the field of space in front of them, but informed his brother that while his imagination was mighty capable, he couldn't see Dec doing a better job than his current copilot, whose skills in her seat were what had located the haystack needle that was Wanten's ship.

"What's your secret, Ymmoss?" AG asked. "Jedi stuff?"

The Gigoran gave him a furry-sounding laugh and then began to explain at length in incomprehensible purring growls, as if she was leaving nothing out, no matter how small the detail—and perhaps, judging by length, also including the history of the details and the far-reaching cultural impacts of that history. It was a long explanation. J-Squadron listened politely, and just when it seemed she would never stop growling, she *still* did not stop growling. Just as Sari gave up hope of the explanation ever stopping—the last of them to do so—Ymmoss finished.

"Well, it doesn't *sound* simple, but if you say so," chided AG, the only one who spoke Gigoran. "I think you're just being modest."

"I do, too, have the Force," Mattis said quietly to himself.

"I know you do," said Cost Niktur, Mattis's space-crazy former cellmate, as she climbed from her hiding place under and behind the weapons console. "I can smell it in you. I come from a race of creatures that can sniff out the Force, and you positively reek of it."

"Really?" asked Mattis breathlessly. Dec hoped Mattis wouldn't put too much trust in what Cost Niktur told him. Even in his short time knowing her, Cost had been incorrect about everything she'd claimed, from the fact that pants were shirts to her ability to understand a single syllable of Gigoran. But Dec could also see that Mattis desperately wanted to believe her. It wasn't enough for Mattis that he *claimed* he was a Jedi. He wanted to prove it to them.

"We're called humans, maybe you've heard of us," Cost told Mattis. "Humans can smell the Force!"

Dec watched as Mattis wilted a little at this flight of fancy from Cost. Just another in a long list. Mattis slumped down onto the weapons console bench. Cost pushed at his feet as she skittered back below and behind the console. She found comfort in tight spaces, and though their ship wasn't the biggest, it had belonged to a Hutt and could reasonably accommodate a Hutt's bulk. It flew pretty fast and was roomier than it looked from the outside. Mattis drew a finger along a control stick and gave it a little push. Through his seat, he felt the gun system on the ship's exterior following the command he hadn't meant to give.

"Way to stay frosty, Mattis," Dec joked, hoping to relieve some of Mattis's gloom.

He didn't get a moment to see if it worked, though, because AG called out, "J-Squadron to battle stations! We're heading into something here, only I'm not sure what."

Lorica took a seat next to Mattis and gave him a confident nod that told him they were about to go into battle together. Dec was glad they were getting along. Heck, maybe they *were* Jedi. Of course, maybe it didn't matter as long as they were friends.

The ship was heading into something, as AG had said, and sure enough, something came into view through the window. From the size and color, it might have been a ship heading for them, only it wasn't exactly a ship. It was a transport, but one that was out of place in this environment. Dec recognized it from their training days, when they had drilled on old Imperial ordnance. What they were looking at was known as an All Terrain Armored Transport, or AT-AT. It was nonoperational, just hanging in front of them in space. AT-ATs were for use on the ground. None of them could guess why or how one was there in the vacuum of space.

AG navigated around the AT-AT to find four more floating there. About fifteen ships, rebel and Imperial both, were scattered among debris from countless other ships. A battle had been fought there decades before. They were flying through a graveyard. Perhaps the vessel that had been transporting the AT-ATs accounted for the debris that plinked off their ship's exterior, sounding like a hailstorm back on Ques. Another inert ship transfixed all of them as it encompassed the entire viewscreen. They'd only ever read about Star Destroyers. Actually seeing something so incomprehensibly big was chilling.

"That's a really big spaceship," Mattis uttered.

"It's possible I am terrified of gigantic things. Starting now."

"That ain't Jedi talk." Dec winked. "And anyway, that Destroyer is as lifeless as the rest of this junk."

"Look alive, everybody," AG barked. "One of these ships looks alive."

A blue-gray dot in the distance was coming in fast. It took seconds to grow enough in view that they could make it out—a First Order TIE fighter, and it was screaming toward them! J-Squadron had recently fought their first ground fight. Now they were engaging in their first aerial combat situation. They had trained for this in sims for a month, but this was real. Time felt thick and sticky. But it was neither, and it stopped feeling slow when the TIE fighter fired off ten shots that shook their ship hard.

"Keep it down!" Cost yelled. "I'm trying to hide!"

Dec shook his head and gathered himself. "AG, that TIE is coming back around for another go. Our shields won't take much more. Make it a challenge!"

"Aye-aye, Brother," AG said, and he spun their

ship and charged the TIE fighter. "They never expect you to charge them."

"Who doesn't?" Sari asked.

"Anyone," AG said.

The TIE fighter dodged at the last second.

"Yeehaw!" AG yelled, weaving through the graveyard.

"No showboating till we're in the clear!" Dec hollered. "But then a lot of showboating," he added. "Find out exactly how much our shields can take, would you, Sari?" he asked with an uncharacteristic lack of snark.

Within seconds, Sari had that information up on her screen and sent it to the display for all to see.

"Snowball, I assume you're keeping an eye on Wanten's ship." Ymmoss yipped what might have been a yes. "Keep it up."

"What do you want me to do, Admiral Handsome?" Cost asked, peeking out from her hiding spot.

"Whatever it is you're doing, keep it up," Dec instructed.

Cost saluted him and tucked herself back under the console.

"You and you," Dec pointed at Lorica and then at Mattis. "Start shooting, will you?"

Mattis and Lorica sprang into action, each firing one of the impressively powerful "boom-bah" cannons on either side of their ship. The Hutt wasn't wrong about the incredible magnitude of their weapons. Boom-bah cannons were named for the sounds they made, a deafening *BOOM* as they were fired, followed by the *BAH* of whatever they hit exploding. Mattis and Lorica fired off *boom*s that rattled their own ship. They missed the TIE fighter completely, and the *bah*s lit up the sky like Marmaconva Borealis during a Harvest Eve festival.

Mattis fired off another four hull-shaking shots. The TIE fighter whipped around Mattis's blasts. It was too nimble a ship. Lorica was waiting for a perfect shot. She pushed her forehead into the scope as hard as she could in the hope that the pressure would help her lock on to the enemy. Two hundred meters past the TIE fighter, an AT-AT exploded. One of Mattis's blasts had finally hit something. It was a start.

Dec shook his head. "I wish we could just throw one of those AT-ATs at it. We'd have a better chance of hitting it. Now *focus*, Mattis."

Dec wasn't sure good leadership was just telling someone to do something and assuming he'd do it, but it seemed to work. He saw Mattis narrow his eyes and line them up with the scope. The back of Mattis's neck was red with concentration. He aimed carefully. He shifted his gun with every movement the TIE fighter made. He waited for his moment. He held his breath. He pulled the trigger. Nothing happened. His gun was depleted. So was Mattis.

"Well," Dec said, "good focus, anyway."

The TIE fighter kept on them, kept hitting them. Soon their shields would be as useless as Mattis's gun. The TIE fighter stayed ahead of Lorica's cannon. It came in closer and closer.

It bore down on them.

It closed in.

This was the end, but not for J-Squadron. The disembodied leg of the exploded AT-AT slammed through the TIE fighter, completely obliterating it.

AG-90 cheered and hollered traditional Ques celebratory exclamations. Dec clapped his brother on the back so hard it sounded like a bell. Sari and Ymmoss hugged. Mattis opened his arms for a hug, but Lorica didn't move. She smiled and pointed to where the TIE fighter had been.

"Lucky," she said.

"Luck?" he gasped. "That was the Force."

"Not *the* Force, Mattis. *A* force," Sari chided, as she only rarely did. "The force from the explosion sending that AT-AT leg through that TIE fighter. Which was also lucky, because this ship is not the equal of a single TIE fighter. . . ." She trailed off, her face frozen in fear. They all looked to the viewport to see what had stopped her.

Another TIE fighter was zipping toward them.

And another.

And a third.

CHAPTER
03

"RUN!" DEC YELLED, by which he clearly meant "Fly as fast as you can away from here right now," and AG completely understood.

He had flown a three-dimensional version of serpentine before, but now AG flew pirouettes, an entire ballet, to dodge the three TIE fighters. He used a cluster of dead X-wings as cover, but no cover lasted long against what felt like thousands of laser blasts.

"There's only one way out of here," Dec said. "Do it." Mattis didn't know exactly what Dec meant by that, but AG did. He shook his head. Sari seemed to know, too.

"No," she said. "AG, you better not."

"Don't be a Gungan. Make the jump," Dec insisted.

Mattis suddenly understood. Dec wanted them to go to lightspeed. It would catapult them out of danger, but it would also mean losing the ship they were following. They'd lose Wanten for good. They'd never see Jo again.

"There's got to be another way," Mattis said.

"There is," Lorica told him, hitting the button that fired her boom-bah. The lead TIE fighter exploded in a fiery ball. Mattis was thrilled, but not for long. The other two TIE fighters flew through the fire.

"Why aren't you shooting, too?" Lorica asked, scanning his station.

"I ran out of ammo," Mattis said.

"Push that to recharge the boom-bah." She pointed at a button. "Flip that to engage your laser cannons." She pointed at a switch above Mattis's head. "When your boom-bah is recharged, that light will go on." She pointed at a bulb at Mattis's eye level.

This was a well-armed ship. Mattis wondered

whether the sims he had done had been poorly armed or if he had missed whole weapons systems during practice. One thing was for sure; the roto-cropper back home had only one weapon on it and it was only good against weeds.

Mattis hit the recharge and activated the laser cannon. The controls popped out of the console. Mattis was embarrassed that he had to be told about the weapons system right under his nose. He tried to shake it off and get firing. He hit the lead TIE fighter! The blasts glanced off its shields, but it was a start. Mattis stopped kicking himself.

AG asked Sari to put the specs for a Star Destroyer up on the screen and warned the gunners not to fire the boom-bahs. Before anyone could ask, AG showed them why. He veered into the hole in the nose of the Star Destroyer and raced through it. The TIE fighters were tight on their tail. If anyone shot a boom-bah in there, they'd all be dead before it had a chance to *bah*.

Their ship was down to its last shields. AG had to outfly the TIE fighters, whose sleeker design and smaller size gave them every advantage. He stayed out of the Star Destroyer's large open spaces for fear of being dangerously exposed. He also kept out of the smaller corridors, as their ship was too big for those and AG needed room to maneuver. AG poured on the speed and shifted direction quickly, often clanging the sides of the ship against the Destroyer's walls. He relied on what shields they had left to withstand those impacts, hoping that the TIE fighters' shields wouldn't be as forgiving. It was a gamble that paid off. AG zigged left, then zagged right into a corridor. The wall clipped a TIE fighter's wing. The pilot tried to eject before his ship exploded, but he was in an enclosed space, so it ended poorly.

The last TIE fighter was too agile for AG's gambit to work a second time. The pilot was too smart. He wasn't pursuing them as aggressively. He hung back, seemingly confident he'd get them eventually.

"Who is this guy?" AG muttered. "Some great pilot? Well, good thing I am, too."

The TIE pilot was letting AG be the one to make the mistake. That was the TIE pilot's mistake. AG floored it. If he could beat the TIE out into space, they could blow the Destroyer and take out their pursuer. The TIE sped up after them, as if the pilot had sensed AG's plan as the droid thought of it.

AG pulled a hard right, a hairpin turn that revealed reflexes faster than any human pilot's. He flew from the corridor into another gigantic ship that had T-boned the Star Destroyer. Due to the angle they'd passed the Star Destroyer initially, Mattis hadn't seen this ship at all from the outside. He couldn't tell from the inside exactly what kind it was. Typical of Imperial design, it was huge and decadent. Windows took up an entire wall. Arches jutted out like sleek steel ribs throughout the room, suggesting that it might have been a transport ship. They might have been in a hangar. Despite the emptiness, it felt oppressive.

AG flew up to the far corner, spun, and hovered facing the way they'd come.

"Gunners, keep your eyes on that hole," Dec instructed, "and when that TIE comes out of it, blast him."

It would have been a good plan if the TIE fighter had played its part. Instead, it smashed through the windows to their right. Shot after shot whittled down what was left of their shields. Mattis returned fire, but he didn't connect. Lorica connected, but it wasn't enough. The last of their shields took the barrage as they flew past the TIE fighter and back out into open space through the shattered window.

Lorica smacked her control stick angrily. Without their shields, the TIE had taken out the laser cannons on both sides. He was dismantling their defenses before finishing them, like a tooka cat playing with a mouse.

"AG," Dec urged, "while we still can," meaning it was time to jump to hyperspace.

"I don't like it."

"I hate it," Dec shot back, "but all I keep thinking is how mad Jo would be if we got ourselves killed for him."

Sari nodded.

"Fire it up, Ymmoss," AG said sadly.

Mattis couldn't believe his ears.

"Better hurry, Snowball," Dec said as that grim gray vessel bore down on them for what, one way or another, would be the last time.

The light in front of Mattis popped on. His

boom-bah was recharged. Those hadn't been clipped. He grabbed the stick and had his finger on the button but stopped himself. Why hadn't Lorica fired her boom-bah? It dawned on Mattis that they were too close to the transport ship. Were he to *boom*, the *bah* would surely kill them all. It was a small victory for Mattis not only to catch up to the present in his thinking but to imagine future consequences of his potential actions. It was a slight consolation with which to leave the world.

Or it would have been, had the TIE fighter not, at that moment, exploded.

It came as a complete surprise. There wasn't a closed mouth on the ship. Ymmoss purred what sounded like a question. AG answered with a shrug. Dec tried to cheer, but he was too confused.

Mattis shook with relief. He felt gratitude to the Force for once again saving them. Wait. Was shooting down a TIE fighter how the Force worked? Maybe. Who else could have saved them? *Poe Dameron,* he thought. Probably Admiral Ackbar had noticed how long they were gone and sent Poe Dameron out of concern. Mattis assumed he soon would see Poe and the rest of Black Squadron. Maybe they had saved Jo already and that's why they'd cut it so close.

Only, Poe Dameron wouldn't be flying the sleek TIE fighter that moved deliberately into view in front of them. This TIE fighter looked newer than the others had and far more sinister, with wings that resembled pincers pointed at them.

"Oh, my gosh, a silencer!" Cost exclaimed, and then ducked back down. From the sound of her scratching around, she was trying even harder than before to hide.

Could Poe Dameron be flying that terrible ship? If so, his rescue mission must have led him down a circuitous path. Mattis knew that his brain was grasping at straws to find a way around the certainty that this new TIE fighter was just coming in to finish the job the others had started. He knew that a ship like this could only be there for one dark purpose.

But why would one enemy ship take out another? he wondered. *On the other hand, why wouldn't it?*

Mattis felt hope slip out of him once again as the deadly TIE fighter bobbed in space in front of them. What was it waiting for? Did it also want to play tooka cat and mouse with them?

Mattis looked at AG, who knew if he so much as moved a centimeter, they'd be blasted out of the sky, and he wouldn't give the TIE the satisfaction. He relinquished the controls and stood up behind Dec, as if the both of them were challenging this enemy ship to finish them off. Ymmoss stood, too, with the same solemn expression. Sari stood. So did Lorica then, and before Mattis knew it, he was on his feet. They were all being brave on their own behalves. Together.

"What's going on?" asked Cost from under some machinery. "Something?" Nobody answered her. J-Squadron stood in stoic silence, bravely daring whatever was coming to come.

The sound of a hailing frequency split the quiet. The enemy ship was calling them. Sari put the call through, and what happened next was unbelievable. A voice they never thought they'd hear again was suddenly all around them.

"Friends! Let me just find the—They're here somewhere. Ah, I think I found—Yes, here it is." They heard a series of clicks. A switch flipped and unflipped, flipped again and flipped right back. "No, that wasn't it. I don't know what that did. Oh, yes. Here we go."

They heard another click and the lights went on in the cabin of the TIE fighter. There at the controls, waving excitedly, was Klimo!

"Did we die?" asked Cost in the stunned silence.

"None of us did," said Mattis, shocked but happy.

They jettisoned a cargo skiff to make room for Klimo's TIE fighter on board their ship. It took Klimo a few tries to find the right button to pop him out onto the deck. The Rodian boy looked mostly as he had—green and rubbery, bulbous in some places and spiny in others. He nervously rubbed his antenna, and Mattis noticed small differences in Klimo's appearance. He had white marks there on the one stalk and on his other hand, and some coming out of his collar on his neck. Scars. There was something else. Klimo used to seem like he was trying to see everything all at once. The world was new and exciting to him. Now he seemed purposeful as he looked

around. Suspicious. The world had nearly killed him. Mattis wondered how much he had changed on the inside.

That is, until Klimo hugged Mattis like a tackleback in a debenball game. He squealed with a joy that clearly hadn't been left behind in a rancor's belly back on Vodran.

"I'm so glad to see you, best friend!" he yelled in Mattis's ear.

Mattis felt himself being squished and lifted. Sari had gathered up both Mattis and Klimo in a giant feet-off-the-floor hug.

"Klimo!" she shouted, seemingly unable to articulate further but getting all her joy and relief into her friend's name. "Klimo! Klimo, Klimo, Klimo!"

With every "Klimo," Sari gave the pair a squeeze and a shake. Klimo might have survived rancors only to die in this hug. When she put them down, Mattis checked to see if anything was broken. Klimo turned to AG.

"You scared us, buddy." AG socked Klimo playfully on the chin.

"I'm glad you're alive." Lorica kissed Klimo on the cheek.

"Me too." Dec kissed him on the other cheek.

Cost, out of her hiding place, approached Klimo gingerly. Klimo regarded her warily.

"I'm Klimo!" he shouted in the friendliest way.

"I'm not!" she shouted back, smiling. "I don't think. But I'm glad you're alive."

"I'm glad you are!" Klimo said, still shouting.

"Can I hug you, too?" asked Cost.

Klimo opened his arms, and Cost rushed into them.

"This is a good hug!" Klimo reported at the top of his lungs.

"I'm glad you like it!" Cost yelled. "I made it for you!"

"Who is this person?" Klimo asked.

Mattis introduced Cost and related how they'd been prisoners together and that an alien creature may or may not have stolen important parts of her mind.

"Speaking of beasts," Klimo said, "let me tell you how I escaped those rancors. It's an amazing story that starts there and gets worse and worse. So many beasts. I had to become one myself kind of, but only after I didn't get to break you out of that prison because you broke yourselves out and then flew away, and there were seven stormtroopers between me and this TIE fighter and I needed it to follow you. That's when I truly became a— That's not where to start the story. The rancors had me. I was finished. But then I thought of something and it saved my life. I thought—" Klimo froze.

His muscles were tense. His hands were fists. He stared past Mattis.

Mattis was confused. He looked where Klimo was looking. There was Ymmoss, mewing to herself, flipping switches on the console. He turned back to Klimo, who was definitely staring at the Gigoran.

"Nobody move," Klimo hissed. "A beast got in here."

Ymmoss spun her chair and looked quizzically at Klimo.

"I think it sees us. Maybe it's not one of the ones you stand still to hide from. Make yourselves as big as you can, everyone!" Klimo stood on his toes and started growling as fiercely as he could.

Ymmoss growled curiously.

"I don't know," AG answered her.

"Stay away from my friends!" Klimo screamed, and charged, leaping at Ymmoss.

Sari caught him in the air. "Klimo. This is Ymmoss. She's a Gigoran and she's our friend, too."

AG nodded. "She's my copilot."

"Yeah, she's his copilot, all right," Dec said.

"Oh. Okay. Sorry. You can never be too careful with beasts," Klimo said. "Anyway. Back to my story of how I got away from all those rancors and the terror of what happened next. You'll never believe what—"

Ymmoss interrupted him with a roar. Klimo tensed again.

"It doesn't sound like she accepted my apology."

"It's not that. In all the din of TIE fighters and getting you back," AG explained, "she's telling us we lost Jo. The ship that took him is gone."

CHAPTER

04

FEW IN THE GALAXY tried to escape their past the way Jo Jerjerrod did, and even fewer failed so spectacularly at it.

Jul and Jax Jerjerrod, Jo's parents, were Imperial loyalists. Jo's grandfather Tiaan climbed the ranks of the Empire until he was named moff. Jo grew up on the Core World of Tinnel IV, as his father and grandfather had before him. Jo was raised to believe in the tenets and ideology of the Empire. He was raised to be the best physically, mentally, and morally and to help those in need. Jo was on a military track before he could walk. His father had called him Grand Moff since Jo was a baby. As the First Order formed, and Jul and Jax rose in the ranks of its Security Bureau, it was clear to everyone that Jo's childhood nickname would end up being prophetic.

Clear to everyone except Jo. Though that wasn't always the case. Until three years before, Jo would have laid the same odds as everyone else in terms of his future. He excelled at school and sports. He sang the anthems the loudest and pledged allegiance the hardest. Even as a child, he was a leader. He wanted nothing more than to make his parents proud. He did his best to embody their ideals. He treated others as he demanded to be treated and would not tolerate those who did any less.

Jo had never met a Gungan before. Gungans rarely left Naboo, but the Boddees were a diplomatic family on Tinnel IV. Before moving into his sector, the Boddees had a river system terraformed into their backyard and, at twelve, Jo was the perfect age to play in a river. So Jo liked the Gungans right away for that reason alone. But the Boddees really won him over when they brought a traditional Naboo gift bucket to every family in the subsector. It was full of brownies that were terrible, what Jo's mother called "an acquired taste." Jo's father called them vegetal. Jo asked if he could show Mr. and Mrs. Boddee's son, Najeema, how they made brownies on Tinnel IV. Najeema hid behind his mother's legs. He peeked out to meet Jo's eyes.

"Would you like that?" Jo asked. "Would you like to try another kind of brownie? I know how to make them," Jo reassured him.

Najeema nodded.

"Come on." Jo ran to the kitchen. Najeema stepped tentatively at first, as if the floor were made of very thin ice. He took a few steps, got a little faster and more confident, and ended up sliding into the kitchen at an excited run.

The two of them made brownies and a mess. It was Jo's first mess. He tried hard to pretend not to like making a mess. When the brownies were ready, Najeema tried one. It was perfect. Crisp on the outside, gooey on the inside. Relentlessly chocolaty.

Najeema hated it. "Too sweet. Needs more broccoli."

He hugged Jo anyway for trying and for being a new friend. Jo realized that it was true; they were friends. Although he had many friends, until Najeema moved there, Jo had never had a best friend.

When Najeema arrived on the planet, he was slight and shy. Jo saw it as his responsibility to make the Gungan comfortable at his new school. Najeema's shyness didn't last the first day. His slightness didn't last the first month. He sprouted quickly, and when Najeema and Jo found themselves on the same junior field grav-crosier team, they dominated. Their team, the Ripper-Raptors, took the trophy that year, and Jo and Najeema shared the Top Player of the Season honor.

Weekends they camped under the stars in one of their backyards, talking and joking and laughing until they couldn't keep their eyes open. Najeema taught Jo how to catch frogs. Mrs. Boddee gave Jo a taste for Gungan stew. Mr. Boddee taught Jo to curse in Gungan.

Their love of games did not stop at field sports. They also played board games, and running games, and hiding games; they played war games and peace games. Jo would say that games taught teamwork and strategy, encouraged sportsmanship and exercise, and that was all true, but he simply loved playing games. Especially with Najeema.

The day Jo and Najeema played Bounty Hunter was when everything changed. Bounty Hunter was a combination of tag, seize the pennant, and hide-and-seek. This round, Jo was the bounty hunter and Najeema was the bounty. Jo tracked him inside, which was good for Jo because he'd hidden the purse, which was the bounty's objective, in a tree outside.

Jo searched methodically. Upstairs first. Jo checked under the beds and in the bathtubs. Najeema wasn't in the bedrooms. He wasn't on the master balcony. He wasn't in the bathrooms. Najeema wouldn't fit in the linen closet, but Jo checked anyway. Najeema sometimes got into places he shouldn't have been able to fit and got stuck. Najeema wasn't in the linen closet. Jo went downstairs. Najeema wasn't in the kitchen, or the living room, or the foyer; he was nowhere to be found. Jo looked in the basement. In the chests. In the closets. Behind the furnace. Under the holo-billiard projector. He couldn't find Najeema anywhere, which was impossible. Jo had tracked him into the house, for certain. Najeema had to be in there somewhere, but Jo had searched everywhere. There wasn't a single room he hadn't checked.

Except there was.

Jax Jerjerrod's study was off limits. It was a place for work, not games. Najeema knew this, Jo was certain. It was one of the many rules of the Jerjerrod house. They'd never gone near his father's study. They'd never been inside, certainly. It wasn't allowed. Besides that, the door was always closed.

But now the door was open. Just a crack.

The first rule Jo had ever broken on purpose was going into his father's study. Najeema was there, looking at something on the desk. When he looked up and saw Jo, he went pale. He seemed to take up less space somehow, as if he were as slight as he had been when he had hidden behind his mother's legs on his first day. Jo couldn't place the emotion, but that look would haunt him. Najeema pushed past Jo.

"Selongabye," he said.

"Selongabye," Jo called after him, confused. The game was over. There would never be another.

Jo told his father what had happened and saw another look that would stay with him forever. His father's face twisted to the point that he became another man. A mean and impatient man. His mother put her hand on her husband's hand, and he softened but only a little.

The next day, Najeema wasn't in school, which was strange. He wasn't at practice, which was even stranger. When Jo got back home, he saw terraformers removing the river system. The Boddees had moved away with neither warning nor trace. They'd given no forwarding information. Jo asked his mother where they'd gone. She told him to talk to his father. Jax was in his study. Jo knocked on the door. He was told to come in and sit down. His father explained that the Boddees had been in their sector acting as diplomats and that the nature of the job was temporary. He wouldn't be surprised if more Gungans came to Tinnel IV soon. They wouldn't necessarily move into their subsector. They wouldn't necessarily have a boy Jo's age. Jax told his son he was sure that once the Boddees got settled, Najeema would get in touch again. He told Jo to go find another friend with whom to play in the meantime, or better yet, spend more time on homework. His father's tone told Jo that the conversation was over.

The Boddees' departure made no sense to Jo. Days before, Najeema had told their grav-crosier coach that he was thinking of switching to a defensive position for the season. Jo and Najeema had talked about costumes for the solstice masquerade. Najeema had been excited for the upcoming field trip to Val Denn; he'd never been to the capital city. There was no way Najeema knew he would be moving away. There were so many reasons why the abruptness of this move raised suspicion in Jo. But none more than the look on his father's face the night before.

He felt as though he saw his father's scowl behind every memory of every plan Najeema had made for the next days, weeks, and months. The back of his neck was sweaty, and his hand shook as he pushed the study door open. He didn't turn on the light. He let his eyes adjust to the dimness. What Jo saw terrified him.

He saw nothing.

His father's desktop was bare. His desk drawers were empty. His shelves were vacant. Everything that had filled the room had been moved, probably to Jax's office in the capital. This was a deliberate countermeasure against Jo. His father no longer trusted him. Well, that distrust was now mutual. The absence of documents was more damning than any evidence of guilt Jo could have found. Whatever it was that Najeema had seen had prompted Jo's father to have the whole Boddee family sent away from Tinnel IV.

Or worse, Jo thought without meaning to.

He couldn't help thinking it. The idea, repugnant though it was, fit with his father's grimace. In the coming months, Jo saw that expression more and more, not just in his father but in the mirror. That glare sent Jo down a new path, one that led him to the Resistance. It led him to where he was now: aboard a First Order *Upsilon*-class shuttle transporting him to his parents to expose his time among rebels. He'd run as far away from his past as he could get. Whole planets. He'd joined an organization whose only goal was to defeat his past, his parents, and the First Order. And now he was being flown right back into the heart of it.

He saw his father's scowl in the face of his captor, Wanten. It wasn't exact, but it was close enough. The derision, the disappointment, the contempt were all on display. The difference was that Jax Jerjerrod had other expressions from which to choose. If Wanten could make another face, Jo had yet to see it. If Wanten was anything but a wounded bully, Jo would be surprised.

Jo ignored Wanten's sweaty gloating. Wanten went on and on about how taking Jo to his parents would get Wanten all the acclaim he always knew he deserved. He groused about his past as the Empire's pariah, but Jo only pretended to pay attention. Instead, he took in every centimeter of Wanten's shuttle, its inhabitants, and the atmosphere outside. He eyed the dashboard. Standard weapons and sensors for this model. Nothing unusual. Room for about five or six in the main cabin, but it was just Wanten, a pilot, a copilot, and Jo. All human. There was a passenger compartment. Two exits. Typical of First Order ordnance, everything was tidy and squared away.

They passed an asteroid field, followed by dead ships from a battle long before. Jo mentally cataloged every icy rock, wrecked ship, and AT-AT out there. Any detail could potentially help him escape.

Jo was confident he could beat Wanten in a fight. Wanten was big but without much muscle. The pilot had neither size nor strength. The copilot, however, had both. She also had a blaster in her hand and half an eye on Jo. If only Wanten hadn't stowed his blaster once they'd taken off, Jo could have taken it off him and taken out the copilot with it. He might only need to threaten them. Could he take the copilot? Not as long as she kept watching him, and it didn't seem like that would change.

The copilot turned in her chair, angling her weapon at Jo and smiling thinly at him. She was meticulously groomed, as was every First Order soldier he'd ever seen. Not a hair out of place. No fat, all muscle. Nearly perfect blue eyes, but for a fleck of brown in the left one. Jo put her in her early thirties, which meant she was likely born around the fall of the Empire. She reminded him of the sweeper on the Imperials, a rival field grav-crosier team. They had the same bearing and nearly the same haircut. That sweeper got into fights often, though she never seemed to care one way or the other about them.

Jo wondered how the copilot had ended up there, dispassionately holding a blaster on him. He wondered if he could change her mind about her allegiances. He bet that he could, but he also knew he wouldn't get the chance.

The copilot seemed to dare Jo to act as she fired up the comms. She looked through Jo as she related that there was a small ship on their tail and requested guidance or assistance. She was told that it would be taken care of. Within seconds, a TIE fighter zoomed out of hyperspace past them. Jo was terrified. He knew J-Squadron's capabilities. He'd written reports on the topic. He wasn't sure they could defeat a TIE fighter in open space.

"That's it?" challenged the copilot. "One TIE fighter?"

Jo realized that this copilot was more like the sweeper than he'd realized. Neither of them initiated fights they had a chance of losing.

"He was a turnaround," the operator said. "Expect three more directly."

Four TIE fighters? Jo banged his fist against his seat, only wishing he'd banged it against Wanten's face. He was certain he could pilot the ship, should he manage a way past his captors. He'd been in an *Upsilon*-class command shuttle once with his mother. Jul got her start as a pilot and liked to keep up to date with the newest ships whenever she was able. The *Upsilon* they had flown was markedly better than this one. This one was closer to the *Lambda*-class T-4a that had inspired it. Jo liked to hear his mother talk about ships. She could go on at length about their aesthetics and mechanics. He had inherited her interest. This was a pretty ship, as well as a powerful one. Its internal hyperdrive was top-of-the-line. A thing of beauty. Jo was relieved the pilot hadn't activated it. His friends never would have been able to follow them if he had.

Also, that the pilot hadn't initiated the hyper-drive meant their destination was close. Jo maintained an accurate mental picture of a star map at all times. He knew their position in space in relation to Vodran. He always tried to know his position in space. If they reached their destination, and he managed to either escape or report, he would be able to direct the Resistance to the location of a First Order base.

If Jo were to overpower them and take control, he could stop the TIE fighters from killing his friends.

Wanten had stopped talking. He was grinning and bouncing in his seat as he looked through the viewports. They were closing in on his victory, and Wanten had a child's excitement. The small wheeze that accompanied his breath and the adjustment of instruments were the only sounds.

In the years after the Boddees disappeared, Jo had turned away from the tenets of his parents and grandfather. But no matter how much he opposed their politics, deep down he wanted his parents to be proud of him. Now they would never be. He felt tears threatening to escape.

Three more TIE fighters rocketed out of hyperspace and past their shuttle. Jo's friends were doomed. Jo realized that he would miss them, and he couldn't help enumerating the order in which that would happen: Lorica, Sari, Mattis, then the other two.

Jo's father's anger boiled inside him. With a roar, he leaped at the copilot and snatched for her weapon.

She was as surprised as he was. Jo grabbed at her blaster as they tumbled to the ship's floor. He landed on top of her, and the blaster fell out of her grip, skidding along the deck. It stopped at Wanten's feet. Jo watched him pick up the blaster.

"DeBoer," Wanten told the copilot, "don't make me blast this boy. He is of greater use to me intact. For now."

The copilot, deBoer, tugged a hank of hair on the back of Jo's head and slammed him face-first into the floor.

It was the sharpest pain he'd ever felt, and he'd had sports injuries that sprained, dislocated, or fractured every one of his limbs at one time or another. The pain in his face was nothing, however, compared to what he felt when the pilot activated the hyperdrive, sending their ship into lightspeed.

CHAPTER
05

YMMOSS PAWED AT buttons and switches all over the control console. She growled low, sounding frustrated.

"She's trying to find the shuttle again," AG translated. "She likes to think out loud, but she's trying not to, 'cause everything she says makes the green one—that's you"—he pointed at Klimo—"jumpier. But it ain't helping her locate Jo any faster or at all. It don't help that our dogfight took out a lot of our systems along with our shields and guns. No long-range communications or you can bet I'd be calling the Resistance for help. Can't believe we didn't do that first thing!"

Mattis watched over Ymmoss's shoulder, wishing he could do more. He sensed that wish in all of them, that they could press against the viewport in hopes of seeing something, anything that would lead to Jo. Only Klimo kept his distance. He seemed scared of Ymmoss. He clutched Cost's hand as if they'd known each other longer than they had and that was something they always did.

Without letting go of Klimo's hand, Cost turned to Mattis and said, "Use force."

"What?" He wasn't unscrewing a jar lid or pushing a hewer through a hemmel field. He couldn't force his way through the stars to find Jo.

"Use force. You stink of it. Can't you smell you? Use force to find your friend."

Mattis realized she was telling him to use *the* Force. Cost had unreliable brains. In the time Mattis had known her, Cost had been wrong about so many things. She slept on the wrong side of the bed: underneath it. Once Cost insisted that the way she breathed was not inhale, exhale, like everyone else, but two at a time. Inhale, inhale, then exhale, exhale. She claimed it saved energy in the long run. She passed out trying to prove it. She was so wrong so often in so many ways, but she was also right occasionally. When she was right, it was about big things. She'd once accidentally betrayed J-Squadron and, rather than allow suspicion to tear them apart, she'd forced her brains together for long enough to confess that she was responsible. So maybe she was right about this. Maybe she could smell the Force on him. Even a clock that has lost track of everything can tell you what time it is sometimes, as long as it still has arms and numbers. And if there was ever a time for it to be one of those times, this was it.

Mattis closed his eyes and hoped Cost was right. He slowed his breathing. He thought about the Force and nothing else. Then out of nowhere, an X-wing flew into his thoughts. Stars lit up the dark canvas of his mental space. He knew he had to focus on the Force and not the X-wing, so he mentally dismantled the ship. He took off each wing and set them aside. He disappeared the body. He turned off the stars one by one, until it was dark. Mattis thought the words *the* and *Force* as loudly as he could. Then he thought the words quieter and quieter. He was getting it now. He had to tell Lorica.

"See what I'm doing?" he asked Lorica. "I'm

closing my eyes. Breathing slowly. Sitting as still as I can. Inside and out, if that makes sense."

"You did great. You made it nearly ten seconds," Lorica said.

"It felt way longer."

"If you really think I'm connected to the Force because of how I used that laser sword, why are you trying to teach me?" she asked him. "Why aren't you asking *me* to teach *you*?"

"That," said Mattis, impressed, "is so smart. That's the kind of thinking that a person with the Force would use. It's brilliant. I feel lightheaded from that."

"You're probably lightheaded from the weird way you were breathing," she responded.

"Please, Lorica," Mattis continued. "Would you train me in the ways of the Force?"

"No," she said, smiling as if she'd said yes. She went back to looking over Ymmoss's shoulder.

"But," Mattis started.

"That's your first lesson," Lorica interrupted.

"How is that a lesson?" he asked.

"Once you figure that out," she said in as serious a voice as she could muster, "you'll be ready for the second lesson."

Mattis shook his head, trying to work out what Lorica meant. He saw Sari had gone behind one of the wings of Klimo's TIE fighter. She crooked her finger to beckon Mattis over.

"While you're doing the Force," Sari started.

"You believe I can do it?" Mattis interjected, breathless. This was exciting. Sari was so smart. If she thought Mattis had the potential to be a Jedi, it was nearly proof that he really did.

She shrugged, then said, "Check on Dec, would you? See if he's all right. I think he's changed since we got back from the robot moon."

"The Force could absolutely help with that," Mattis said, beaming. "But Dec seems like himself to me."

"Something's different, and I can't put my finger on it," Sari said. She asked Mattis if he'd noticed the distance she'd observed between Dec and AG.

They peered around the TIE to see that Dec and AG were hugging.

"Sorry if I was a sore-head," Dec said. "It just hit me sideways to not sit next to you, but the fluffball is a better copilot than I ever was. I wouldn't have tried half the stuff she did."

Ymmoss purred.

"You forgive me?" Dec asked AG.

"Kin can be sore at kin?" AG asked, stunned.

"Sure, sometimes," Dec said.

"I didn't know kin could be sore at kin," AG said. "And you were sore at me even though I didn't actually provoke it or know about it or know it was possible or anything?"

"Yeah, but I ain't anymore," Dec said.

"You," AG repeated, "were sore at me."

Dec nodded, abashed.

"Even though I'm me," AG clarified. A circuit in his robot mind seemed blown. "And you're you. You were sore."

"But I intend not to ever be again ever, I swear," Dec promised.

Sari rested her hand on the TIE's wing and sighed.

"Okay," she said. "But see? He *was* mad, even if he's not anymore."

She pointed out how Dec had just taken charge of the unit, when authority was something he'd theretofore either shirked or challenged.

"Dec seems to care about Jo now. That doesn't seem strange to you?" she asked.

"I don't know," Mattis said. "He cares about his kin, and J-Squadron's kind of become kin, haven't we? Even Jo? And yeah, Dec challenges authority, but he's always kind of been in charge, don't you think?"

From the first time they met, Dec was always running one scheme or another. He had that kind of mind and a way about him such that regardless of whether he meant to lead or not, people followed. Sari moved to look back around the TIE at Dec, but he'd come over and was only centimeters away from her.

"So pretty, ain't she?" Dec regarded the sleek TIE fighter. "I know it's a weird thing to admire the enemy's ship, but the TIEs are a far cry from the junked-together jumble-skis, fan-shuttles, and sail-crafts that skipped along the glades back on Ques."

Mattis nodded. The TIE fighter really was an impressive ship. Dec waved his hands to shoo them.

"Move out of the way. I had a flash of brilliance is what. A notion to hop in this here TIE and fire up her instruments. Use 'em to get a bead on Jerjerrod. Takes an enemy ship to catch one, maybe. Smart, I know. Save the parades, though. Let's get our boy back."

As Dec boarded, Sari angled her head at him, as if his sentiment was more evidence of a change. Mattis shrugged.

"She's already purring," Dec yelled from inside. "Has she been on this whole time? Klimo? I can't believe how quiet she runs." Dec leaned half outside the ship. "And how cool. Any other ship'd be burning up hot. We'd feel the heat of her this close. She is some machine, hoo-wee! Gotta get me one!"

"You can have that one!" Klimo yelled. "I'm finished using it."

Dec ducked back inside and after a series of audible clicks, he let out the worst curse they have on Ques.

"No, no no no! No! Come on, you hunk of junk!"

Dec leaped out of the TIE and smacked it on its side.

"She's out of power from idling. You didn't hear her turn off, though, did you? She's so quiet, she shut off just now and you didn't even notice!

Sounds the same on and off! Which is amazing. I can't stay mad at her, she's such a great little ship!"

Klimo apologized, explaining that in the excitement to see his friends, he must have forgotten to power down the TIE. He'd been coasting the whole way after them. He'd stolen the ship from a refueling station before the pilot could refuel it.

"I had a hat like that once," Cost said, trying to console him. She squeezed his hand.

"Better figure something else out," Dec said with a sigh. "Nothing the TIE can do for us now."

"Come on." AG nudged Sari. "Let's get her running, prove Dec wrong."

"Prove me wrong? What? That ain't like you, Brother. What's—" Dec started to ask, but AG was inside.

The TIE was as impressive inside as out. Sari and AG gaped at the tech.

"She really is a sweetheart," AG said and whistled like the astromech he partly was.

Ymmoss roared a suggestion demurely.

"Hey, yeah, that could work," AG said. "Figure we don't need the engine to turn over. We just need to power it enough to get the systems online." AG tapped his chin, making a *tink-tink* sound, then leaped around Dec, grabbing cables and connecting the Hutt ship to the TIE.

Dec nodded. "All we probably need to access are her charts or signals."

"Yeah, that was Ymmoss's point," AG said.

"I'm glad she agrees with me," Dec said as he helped divert power to the sleek little ship.

After the beating their ship had taken from the TIE fighters, Dec was pleased that it was able to provide for the First Order ship in far better condition. He was proud of their junker. It was a very Ques sort of ship. No matter how exciting the TIE was to look at, Dec would always prefer to fly in an underdog.

"There you go," he told their ship as the TIE came back online. "Good job."

Dec fired up the TIE's systems and felt only the smallest pang of guilt for admiring its interior once more. Not only was it really remarkable, but the interface was completely intuitive. Dec quickly found the coordinates from the TIE's last known heading, which would return them to its base of origin, where Wanten was taking Jo.

Dec felt even guiltier when their ship sputtered and shook through the leap to hyperspace. It was low on fuel and shields and everything else, and Dec nearly doubted they would make it through to the other side, but it held.

They emerged from hyperspace. Dec scanned the sky for Wanten's ship. He wondered how far behind they were.

Mattis gasped and pointed out into space. "Will you look at that."

Outside the viewscreen, a glowing horizon line lit the sky. A band of red light that was at once beautiful and horrible. Ymmoss mewled. So did Cost.

"A giant laser," Lorica said. "It's coming from that moon over there."

"Is that a moon?" asked Dec.

Mattis's thoughts raced. He knew what it was. He had heard about this weapon in the histories of the space battles that had come before.

"That's a Death Star."

"Oh. Of course, sure, okay," said Dec. "What's a Death Star?"

"The Empire built weaponized planets to destroy the rebels," Mattis said. "Not once but twice."

"Looks like the First Order copied them," Sari said.

"Then you bet your biscuits that's where that First Order rat took Jo to his First Order rat parents," Dec said. "Full speed ahead, Captain Ninety."

AG saluted sarcastically. Dec raised a curious eyebrow.

"We need to report to the Resistance," Lorica said. "I'm sure everyone in the galaxy saw that beam and is wondering where it came from. We need to tell them about this laser planet, about Jo. I know our long-range communications are out, but how are our short-range?"

"Good idea," Dec said as Ymmoss scanned the communications frequencies. "Maybe we can figure out a way to bounce a signal or—"

"Starkiller Base requesting landing code." A voice filled their ship, revealing that, unfortunately, the short-range communications were in working order. "Please respond. This is our final request. State your landing code immediately. Fail at your peril."

A panic followed. A din consisting of "We gotta get out of here" and "What do we do," some low roaring from the copilot, as well as "Someone think of something" and a single "Let me think of something" from Sari. Cost yelled about all the yelling, and Klimo yelled that it was all going to be fine because of friends and friendship. Lorica didn't speak, because her brain was too busy darting from the start of one plan to the next, in search of a strategy that might not be doomed. Dec didn't speak, either, because he had come up with a plan that he thought would succeed. He raised his hand and closed his fist the way he'd seen Admiral Ackbar do in the mess hall to silence the troops. It worked; the group fell silent. Dec activated the communicator and confidently rattled off a series of numbers.

There was a long frozen silence.

"Landing code accepted. You're cleared for landing. Hangar two-thirty-two. Park in the back."

Dec took his finger off the communicator and exhaled his relief.

"I can't believe that worked," he said. "That was a total guess."

"What!" Mattis exclaimed. He couldn't believe it.

"Way our day's gone, we were bound to turn up some luck eventually."

Sometimes Mattis thought that everyone in J-Squadron already had the Force.

"I know what you're thinking," Dec said. "That I might have the Force."

"How did you know that?" Mattis asked. "Is it because you have it?"

"No, it's because that's what you're always thinking. I was just messing with you. I don't have the Force. I do have a note full of landing codes I got from the cockpit of Klimo's TIE fighter."

Dec showed the note. Sari laughed in a way that was unusually light for her. Dec checked to see if AG was laughing.

"Everyone buckle up," the droid instructed. "We're coming in for a landing."

Klimo strapped in Cost first and then himself. Mattis strapped in beside Sari, who he saw was staring at Dec.

"Why are you staring at me?" she finally said, without turning toward Mattis.

"Why are you staring at Dec?" he asked.

"That call sign business," she told him. "Dec mischief."

"See?" Mattis said. "He hasn't changed."

Sari nodded. "I guess not."

"Maybe you have," Mattis said, trying to sound wise.

"Can I tell you something, Mattis?" she asked, finally turning away from Dec to look at him.

"Anything," he replied. "Always."

"I think I *have* changed." She looked down, then up, and her face flushed pink. Whatever she was about to tell him was difficult for her. Mattis tried to give himself soft eyes and to make his face inviting and nonjudgmental. "Why are you making that face?"

"Soft eyes," Mattis said.

"You're so weird."

"I know. What did you want to tell me?"

Sari gave him a goofy grin. "I think I like Dec," she whispered. Then, in an effort to bury her words with more words and not give Mattis an opportunity to reply, she explained, "It's a crush! And I'm only telling you because we might land on that Death Star and get killed by stormtroopers, so I just wanted to say it out loud and hear how it sounded, and it sounds stupid, so never mind."

Mattis smiled at his friend. "It doesn't sound stupid," he told her.

"We're landing," she said.

They watched the planet's surface become visible as they entered its atmosphere. It was mostly white, mountains and valleys covered in ice and snow.

"Look at that." Mattis pointed at a dingy, flat wreck of a vessel parked on a cliff.

He thought it looked like a robot's skull, if robots had skulls.

"I wonder why a Corellian freighter came here to die," AG said as he steered past it toward the forest below.

Mattis perked right up and saw Sari do the same. They spoke excitedly back and forth about how they knew a Corellian freighter from the stories they'd heard growing up, but neither had ever seen one before. They tried to discern if this one might be the one they'd heard about, but there was no way to tell as they soared past it.

They landed softly in a thatch of trees. They

had been cleared to land in the hangar, but AG thought it better not to push their luck.

Before entering the unknown of what they had come to learn was called Starkiller Base, they raided both the Hutt's ship and Klimo's stolen TIE fighter for any supplies they could find. They found a good amount of rations. Harra the Hutt had an appetite for dried meat sticks. Mattis thought they tasted better when he didn't know just what kind of meat it was. A spare uniform in the TIE only fit AG, which would have drawn attention. Sari found a screen-card in the pocket, however, that proved useful. It didn't take much slicing to map out the base. Lorica found com-links in the Hutt's ship. She passed them out and laid out their missions.

AG, Klimo, Cost, and Ymmoss were to secure a fully gassed-up ship for the getaway. They would need something fast that would hold everyone. Lorica, Dec, Sari, and Mattis would find Jo. Sari pulled up the grid on the screen-card. She showed AG and Ymmoss the route to sneak into a hangar. AG loaded it into his memory and led his team off.

"Good luck, Brother," Dec called after AG.

AG didn't respond. Had he not heard it? Impossible. He had perfect hearing.

"You too," AG finally said.

"Maybe I should go with them." Dec looked worried. "AG might be glitching."

"I know the feeling," Sari said. When Dec furrowed his brow at that, she added, "Never mind."

Mattis nodded sagely.

"I'm running fine. You lead your team. I'll lead mine," AG called, with an edge to his voice that Mattis had never heard before. The easygoing droid hadn't let any sharpness come into his speech even when they all thought they were staring down death earlier.

Sari showed Dec, Lorica, and Mattis the safest way to the Jerjerrod living quarters. As strange as it was to be on a world engineered to destroy them, it was even stranger to see their friend's name located in the center of an enemy map.

CHAPTER

06

JO WOKE ON A COUCH in a room he didn't recognize, but he'd been in many just like it. He knew the room, despite never having been in that particular one. It was spare and utilitarian. It was gray. It could only be a First Order room.

It took a second for his eyes to focus. It took another before the pain hit. An angry stripe up the bridge of his nose spread out to his forehead. There was something sharp and cold on top of the pain. He reached for it.

"Don't," his father said.

Jax Jerjerrod looked concerned. He looked

older, too, Jo thought. They'd spoken recently enough on the vidcoms but hadn't seen each other in person in two years. Jax cautioned Jo not to move the ice pack from his brow in a voice both thinner and kinder than Jo remembered.

For a moment, Jo thought he'd imagined everything. His father's concern seemed genuine. His face seemed incapable of the dark turn of expression that haunted Jo. Had Jo gotten everything wrong? A panic swelled in him that surged and produced a sheet of embarrassment that warmed his chest and made him perspire from chin to collarbone.

"All right then, Grand Moff Jerjerrod." Jax sighed, kindness ebbing. "Let's hear it. Are you with the Resistance? Really?"

Jo's breath came fast. His panic subsided only to reemerge and leave him gasping.

The door slid open. His mother entered in a pristine uniform. Jul Jerjerrod looked elegant and deadly; the whetstone of years had sharpened her. She looked at her husband and, pointedly, not at Jo.

"Well," she said. "Is he with the Resistance?"

"I just asked him," Jo's father said wearily.

"And what did he say?"

"He hadn't answered yet and then you came in and here we are."

"Is it true? Is that sweaty career-long failure Wanten right?" She finally looked at her son. "Are you with the Resistance?"

Jo tried to read his mother's expression, but it was unreadable. Unemotional. Like the copilot on the shuttle to this base. Like the room. All of it was First Order through and through.

"Answer your mother," his father said, but Jax Jerjerrod's voice made it plain that he didn't want to hear the answer at all.

Shortly after the day he'd played Bounty Hunter as a kid, Jo's performance at school had declined. He'd started accruing aggression penalties on the grav-crosier pitch. Coach Karthata sent him to the grand counselor, Rees Rishikesh. Jo hadn't been the kind of student to be sent to the grand counselor before, but he had been acting like an entirely different kind of student.

Jo thought Rishikesh's office was strange. It felt like twilight somehow. The rest of the school was bright and angular. Rishikesh's office was softer but not weaker. It was stronger for its difference. It was safe, somehow isolated and secure. Rishikesh, too, was different. The rest of the academy's staff demanded excellence above all things. Rishikesh didn't care about that. He prized what Jo felt over what he did.

Jo was flailing. His best friend was gone. His parents weren't who he thought they were. Grades and sports had been important, but now they felt small, and their previous importance felt like vanity. The foundations of his world were untethered. His teachers and his coach wanted him to pretend that everything was as it had been, but everything wasn't and he couldn't. Rishikesh didn't want Jo to pretend. He didn't want Jo to be who he'd been. Rishikesh listened to Jo. Rishikesh tried only to understand him. He wanted Jo to become who he would be.

Jo desperately missed his life of principle and order. Rishikesh helped him come to terms with the idea that the principles hadn't been his. The order he'd enjoyed had come from outside.

"You must find your own principles," Rishikesh told him. "Make your own order."

Over the year that followed, Rishikesh helped Jo immensely before recruiting him for the Resistance. With Rishikesh's direction, questions, and protection, Jo found his own principles. They resembled those of his upbringing, in the way that a tree resembled a sketch of a tree. Rishikesh taught Jo not to settle for the drawing. He showed Jo how to plant his own tree and to nurture and grow it. To find his own truths and to live them. Jo aspired to the sincerest expression of the best tenets of his upbringing: to lift up those who needed it, to find and facilitate the best in people.

To the cruel and ambitious, the principles of the Empire were a means to an end. They were a management strategy to keep those who toiled for the powerful working as hard as they could be made to. Those who didn't bolster the power structure were of no use. Those who dared work against it were the enemy. Get in line or else. That's how the Empire ruled the galaxy. The First Order inherited the lies of the Empire. It would use up those who served it and destroy any who opposed it.

Like Jo, the Resistance believed in both the individual and the team. It believed that a person lost nothing by elevating those around him or her. That, in fact, everyone rose high from such efforts. Jo was proud of his beliefs and of his determination to live them. After finding moral kinship with the Resistance, Jo qualified as a pilot. He turned down command of a ship, however. He preferred to work with fresh recruits. He liked training them and helping bring out their best qualities. He was proud of his efforts with J-Squadron and prouder of their efforts under him. He was even proud of Dec, who'd always given him so much trouble.

"Yes," he said to his parents, in their gray uniforms in their gray quarters. He told them with strength and pride, his panic subsiding, "I am with the Resistance and the Resistance is with me."

"That ends now," his mother said.

Jo's panic returned as if it were an obedient pet his mother had called.

"Was this our fault? We encouraged him to make his own way," his father fumed. "Or is this that new grand counselor's fault? Strayed from tradition, that one. A lack of respect at the head, what do you expect from the body?"

Jax's expression went darker, nearing the one that had haunted Jo.

"Or was it those blasted Gungans?"

His father's invoking Najeema and his family turned Jo's panic into anger.

"It's your fault," Jo whispered. Then he yelled, "It's your fault! You put the First Order first and your family second. And for what?"

"The First Order *is* your family," his mother said calmly. "You will be loyal to both. You will give up this Resistance foolishness. You will live here with us. Until we figure out exactly what to do with you, you're not to leave these quarters. And do not yell at your father."

"I'll need to fill out a report," his father said. "Tell them the nature of this relationship. And that we'll have a third in our residence."

"Don't bother," Jo seethed. "You're my parents. I'll always want to make you proud, and I'll always love you, but I have to live my own life. You can't keep me here. I don't accept your authority over me."

"What do you think we're going to do?" his father asked. "Give you a ship? Send you on your way?"

"I won't pack him a lunch," his mother said, turning away. She turned back to face Jo. "I won't pack you a lunch."

"I didn't think you would! I'm not asking you to!"

"You had better not walk out that door!"

"You can't keep me here, Mother! What are you going to do, freeze me in a block of carbonite?"

"You are our son and you are grounded," she informed him. "If you choose not to abide by the rules of this family, you will not be afforded its protections."

"I don't need your protections!" Jo yelled, aware of his volume.

"Don't," his father said, also aware.

"You've never needed them more, Jo; you'll see. You will be treated as a member of the Resistance and punished by the First Order, which will entail entirely different paperwork for your father. Now sit down."

Jo refused to sit. There was no way she could make him obey her.

His mother reached for her blaster.

CHAPTER

07

AG WAS SORE at his brother. He wasn't sure if he was doing it right. He'd been sore at other folks, but mostly for being on the wrong side of his kin. He'd never been sore at kin before. There was a first time for everything—so far anyway. He saw how the edge he'd put in his voice had shaken Mattis, too. AG hoped Mattis didn't think he was sore at him. He wasn't. But Dec and Mattis had been standing next to each other, and maybe AG's aim was off.

He was sore at Dec for being sore at him before. AG hadn't done a thing! Being on the receiving end of a good strong dose of mad stung more than a little bit. It all stung. Everything stung. He hated being sore in general, but being sore now, at Dec, really got AG's goat.

It was harder to be sore when Dec wasn't around to receive the brunt of it. AG didn't know what to do with his anger or where to put it. It wouldn't work to act prickly with Klimo or Cost; they wouldn't understand it. He couldn't bear to grump or snipe at Ymmoss. She was very sweet and was helping as best she could in dangerous circumstances that had little to do with her.

At first, when Dec had taught AG to ride a scoot-bike around the quarry near their patch of Ques, Dec had been the captain. AG just rode on the back and observed. His knee bolts had shaken against the scoot-bike's rumbling chassis, but he learned the handles, buttons, and pedals. When AG felt comfortable having a try at being captain, Dec rode on the back. AG took to it quickly, and Dec stayed aft for months, until their mom salvaged enough parts to heap together a second scoot-bike. AG aimed to send his bad mood to ride in the back of his attention until it was time to reckon with it. It would still be there, but in the meantime, AG would be the scoot-bike captain and navigate his team through Starkiller Base.

AG's senses were as good as his reflexes. He kept Klimo, Cost, and even Ymmoss out of the way of stormtroopers on patrol. He didn't know he should have done a better job of keeping the stormtroopers away from Cost.

AG's team was making its way toward what his uploaded map called an atrium. AG pulled everyone into an alcove with plenty of time to avoid a stormtrooper on patrol. AG was confident that the stormtrooper helmet provided terrible peripheral vision and that he and his friends were safe as houses. AG saw everything start to tumble out of control at a reduced rate of ocular sensory intake. He noticed Cost was about to give voice to her terror. And anytime Cost gave voice to anything, it was loud and mostly nutty. Fortunately, just as on the ship, Ymmoss acted as copilot, seeing what AG saw just as he saw it. And as on the ship, she acted quickly and without having to be told. She put a hand over Cost's mouth to keep her from revealing and endangering them. She carried Cost away from the atrium to the back of the alcove.

Ymmoss kept Cost quiet but not calm. AG imagined that it must have seemed like her fears had sprung up and grabbed her by the face, poor thing. Her eyes tried to find what it was that had stopped her mouth from calling out. She squirmed and wriggled. Ymmoss tried petting Cost's head with her other hand to soothe her. It worked, or seemed to. Cost got quiet, went still, then limp. She was playing dead. Poorly. She opened one eye to assess the effect of her performance. Ymmoss smiled at her. Cost started thrashing around again in alarm.

Of course Klimo was set off by all this. Before the little Rodian could make a run for Ymmoss and pry at her enormous hand with his thin sausage fingers, AG grabbed his shirt.

"No no no," Klimo said, getting louder and louder.

AG forced a casual affect as he leaned out into the concourse, as if that would keep him from being spotted. No stormtroopers had heard them. Yet. This needed to be contained. If Klimo worked himself up into a yell, it would all be over. And nobody worked himself up into a yell like Klimo.

AG understood that Cost's experience with stormtroopers on Vodran was what made her fearful. He understood that Klimo's experience with aggressive, carnivorous megafauna on Vodran made him fearful, too. He understood both those things but couldn't find sympathy for either of them. What he knew and what he felt were at odds. The memory of Dec was there on the back of the scoot-bike, dragging its feet because it liked the sound they made against the gravel. Dragging everything out of whack. AG focused on the most important part of being captain: control.

"Klimo," AG said. "We're pals, right?"

That got Klimo's attention. Klimo loved his friends and relished the opportunity to declare it.

"Of course," Klimo said.

"Good. I need your help. Somebody needs to talk Cost off the ledge she's up on before she falls off it. Get me?"

"Kind of," said Klimo.

"*Somebody* is you."

Klimo nodded. "Got it."

AG let Klimo go, smoothed his shirt, and sent him on his way with a "Go get 'er" and a pat on the bottom.

"Cost," Klimo said, more calmly than he'd ever said anything in his life. He was clearly having trouble maintaining that calm. "May I speak with you for a moment?"

Cost also quieted down, as if a switch had been flipped. If only they made switches like that, thought AG. He imagined the blueprints. Detailed designs for switches to calm humans cycled through his mind, but he couldn't figure out the bioengineering aspect. It would take dedicated thinking to work out how to link the mechanized to the organic, and AG didn't want to let his attention stray. He wasn't Mattis.

"I know what it's like to be scared," Klimo told Cost. "Because of the times I've been scared. I remember those times. That's how I know what it's like. Do you know what kept me from letting my fear get the better of me?"

"Rectangles?" Cost guessed, then corrected herself. "No. Squares!"

"It wasn't a shape," Klimo told her. "It was realizing that if the thing that was making me scared made me *act* scared, the thing would eat me. And then it would win. And I couldn't let it win. In my case, the thing was exactly four hundred and twelve monsters. In your case, it's some stormtroopers."

"I don't want store trumpets to eat me," Cost admitted.

AG could not believe this was working, but it was.

"What I did instead of being scared was count the monsters. It might be too loud to count stormtroopers now though. But whenever one of us is scared, because of stormtroopers or because of this monster that we hang out with now for some reason"—Klimo gestured at Ymmoss, shaking his snout and shivering his antenna—"we should squeeze each other's hands or poke each other in the shoulders."

Cost nodded gravely. "Like triangles would."

"Exactly." Klimo smiled.

Ymmoss shrugged. She couldn't believe it was working, either.

Three stormtroopers marched by without incident. They didn't notice a droid or a furry behemoth. They didn't notice a weird little being poking an equally weird little Rodian in the shoulder sixteen or seventeen times.

After what felt like long enough, AG stuck his head out. It was quiet as a morning marsh after a rain. No stormtroopers anywhere. To get where they were going, they needed to go up about sixty stories. It was time to start climbing.

AG had been leading them to an elevator, which was a calculated risk, but when he saw how the walls had been built, he decided climbing was safer. There were notches every few meters that AG assumed were functional and technical, but they reminded him of handholds and footholds. Maybe it was an emergency exit system in case of fire. Maybe it was an invitation provided by some disgruntled First Order designer to any invaders to sneak around via the walls.

Ymmoss mewled about finding another way up. It was her size that worried her. She would be very visible, even more than she already was. AG reassured her that nobody would be dense enough to be on the wall of a shielded secret base in the first place, and therefore nobody would be looking for anyone there. Furthermore, he explained his theory that there was no way stormtrooper masks could allow for much peripheral vision. Nobody would be able to spot them unless they knew to look, and nobody knew to look. The wall of Starkiller Base was probably the safest place to be.

Cost took right off, as if she was born to travel vertically. AG kept an eye on her so she didn't get so far ahead that it would cause problems. He didn't want to have to call out to her, nor did he want to climb extra floors to retrieve her. Every time she'd get too far, he'd let out a little whistle and she'd stop and wait for them.

A strange thing happened about five hundred meters up. A human person was climbing down. She couldn't have been much older than any of them.

AG thought they'd been caught, but only for a second. He realized that this human was sneaking around just like they were. There was no way the First Order would bother with a freelance undercover security climber, though it appeared that they ought to have invested in one. Starkiller

Base was practically crawling with people crawling its walls.

AG nodded to her as anyone would nod as they passed a stranger sharing the same patch of unlikely space. Keep it quiet and go on your way. She nodded back. Polite. Quiet. Quiet was the key.

"Hello!" yelled Klimo at his quietest volume, which was very loud. "Climbing around, too, huh?"

She ignored him, which was good.

AG hushed him, but Klimo couldn't hear it over his own yelling. "Are you sneaking around? We're sneaking around."

"Keep going," AG whispered sternly underneath Klimo.

The girl climbed away from them fast.

"I guess you're just keeping going! We'll do that, too. Bye!"

"Do not wave good-bye, Klimo. You will fall off this wall."

"That rhymed," observed Klimo, who kept climbing and did not, despite his terrible odds, end up falling to his death at all.

CHAPTER

08

LORICA SENT DEC ahead to scout the way, as he had proven the best sneak any of them had ever known. Lorica, also excellent at stealth, followed closely enough to keep him in her line of sight. Sari was hard to hide due to her size. Mattis could only be relied on for intermittent furtiveness. They brought up the rear. They kept Lorica in view as she found the next alcove, closet, or hallway big enough to hide them. She signaled, and they raced to her. And so it was that J-Squadron slowly, strategically, and methodically invaded Starkiller Base.

Mattis and Sari hid behind a beveled steel column. Sari had her back against it, and Mattis stood in front of her so he could see Lorica. Mattis noticed Sari's expression was one he'd never seen on her before. She looked the way he had felt back on Durkteel, when he yearned to be a pilot but didn't know if he'd ever get farther off the ground than the roto-cropper.

Lorica signaled, and they crept to the safety of a technologically impressive alleyway. Even masked in shadow, Mattis could see that Sari's expression remained abstractly sad. Lorica ran off once more.

"What are you thinking about?" Mattis asked.

Sari looked caught, as if she hadn't considered how her thoughts would show on her face.

"Honestly, I'm thinking about how I couldn't sleep on D'Qar." She sighed after a moment. "When I first got there, I mean. I couldn't sleep. I'm from a planet called Baraan-Fa."

"I've heard of Baraan-Fa," Mattis said. "They have that bazaar. It's supposed to be the best."

"Exactly so," she said. "Where I grew up, on the outskirts of the market, the birds would start at sundown. The small ones first, the titterlings and spollows, chirruping in short bursts back and forth in imitation of each other. Kollowaries would hoot low. The shonserras would coo these elaborate melodies that the tench doves would whistle over and around. It was an orchestra. You couldn't help but breathe the rhythm of it, which would send you off to sleep where you'd dream the music, too."

Mattis had seen pictures of most of those birds in his books. He found himself wishing he could fall asleep to the sounds of them, too.

Lorica waved. Mattis couldn't tell if she had just started waving or had been at it awhile and he just hadn't noticed. The way she pushed them into a corner then down into a squat told him that he'd probably kept her waiting. They'd barely steadied themselves when Lorica bounced away from them and off again.

"D'Qar was a green enough planet," Sari said. "There were plenty of birds."

Mattis nodded eagerly. "We saw those castua cranes once."

"Yes, and we'd get birds in the base some-times, just flying through or honking at a droid, or squawking during announcements."

"I once saw a blue dressto perched on an X-wing. Did I ever tell you that? It looked like it was judging our ships, like 'You call these wings?'" Mattis smiled at the memory.

"Plenty of birds on D'Qar." She sighed again. "But nothing nocturnal, not that I could hear. No lullaby."

Mattis held a finger to his lips. Sari stopped talking. Mattis pointed to a mouse droid rolling toward them. Mattis held his breath, hoping not to be noticed. It bounced off his foot. Hard.

"Ow!"

From nearly ten meters away, he heard Lorica shush him.

"Sorry," he whispered loudly. Lorica shushed him again.

Mattis kicked the mouse droid, no longer caring whether it noticed him. It squealed and rolled away, mumbling in beeps and boops.

"I never really fit in on Baraan-Fa," Sari said.

"Because of your size?" Mattis asked.

"No," she said. Sari told him that everyone on Baraan Fa was about a size and a half bigger than most people tended to be. If anything, at only a

size bigger than most, she was small for her planet. She told him she didn't fit in because of something else completely: She lacked a killer instinct. She couldn't *sell* anything. Life on Baraan-Fa was lived in service to the Harvest, which was what the locals called the bazaar.

"The Harvest felt so exciting, like going into hyperspace," Sari told Mattis. "The whole community would come together to think of new and exciting goods. We'd help each other execute the wildest ideas. We aspired to beauty and strangeness. When a stall sold out, the cheers would spread all the way to the ends of the marketplace! Collaboration made us thrum and thrive. I loved it more than anything. But that it was all about money felt empty in the long run. I wanted more. It took me a while to figure out what it was that I wanted, but I'm nothing if not analytical. Ultimately, I realized I wanted to see what a people could be, to see what a people could do, rather than to see what a people could sell. That's why I joined the Resistance."

The mouse droid rolled back toward them with a bigger mouse droid behind it. They headed right at Mattis, beeping angry threats. Sari scooped them both up. She held the bigger one in her armpit while she popped open the smaller one.

"But I didn't fit in there, either," she said, slicing into the memory patch of the smaller mouse droid. "This time it was because of my size. I was seen as a brute, a bruiser. Not only was there no soothing chorus of birds to play me a good night"—she shook her head and sent the little mouse droid on its way—"my bed was too small. Either my legs hung off the end or I'd lay on my stomach, bend my knees, and lay my shins against the wall, which is no way to sleep."

"Terrible," Mattis said, imagining how hard it would be to sleep without a bed fully underneath him. "You didn't fit."

"Exactly so." She popped open the bigger mouse droid, which squealed in protest. "I got really homesick. I realized how much love I held for Baraan-Fa after all. I finally understood that while it may not have been perfect, it shared many qualities with perfection and the rest were to be aspired to, not sought after elsewhere."

The mouse droid continued to squeal. Sari

scowled at it, closed its casing, then smashed it against the wall. It stopped squealing. From a distance, Lorica shushed them again.

"That realization brought me to another one," Sari said as she popped its shell back open. She concentrated for a moment on the mouse droid. Satisfied, she closed it up and set it on the ground. It whistled a friendly good-bye and rolled after its friend.

Mattis was struck by Sari's ability to relate her story and reprogram droids she'd never seen before at the same time. He added her to his list of friends who might have the Force and not realize it. He couldn't remember if he'd already had her on the list. He made a note to write down the list rather than keep it in his head. He started to imagine what sorts of things he'd like to do once the Force manifested for him, when he realized that Sari was continuing her tale. Mattis snapped back to attention.

"The First Order is a threat to everything," Sari said. "Including Baraan-Fa. My home planet is an oasis. It's mostly stayed outside of galactic conflict. It might not always be that way. It might not have a choice. I want Baraan-Fa to stay safe. That's worth fighting for."

Mattis didn't have much love for Durkteel but longed to visit planets that would mean as much to him as Sari's did to her.

"I loved my home enough to want to fight to preserve it," Sari said, "and yet missed it so much I might have to leave the fight to return to it."

"So you're feeling homesick again." Mattis connected her story to his initial question. "I get it."

Sari smiled. "No, Mattis. I'm distracted because of the thing I told you on the ship. I like Dec. And that's just got me thinking of everything in the galax—"

Lorica came running at them fast, interrupting. She waved and whisper-yelled "Go go go!"

Sari and Mattis stood and broke into a run. Lorica and Dec overtook them and led them farther down the corridor and nearly out the other end. Lorica grabbed Mattis before he was able to run all the way out. He caught a glimpse of what had sent Lorica and Dec running. Fifty feet away, walking down a main corridor perpendicular to theirs, were stormtroopers. What looked like hundreds of them.

"Did they just get out of a meeting?" Dec grouched.

"Do you think stormtroopers have pep rallies?" Lorica whispered.

Thousands of boot steps pounded a deadly rhythm that echoed all around them.

Mattis was surprised to realize that despite the palpable danger, because he was standing shoulder to shoulder with Lorica, he felt brave. Maybe she was manipulating his emotions in her Zeltron way. Maybe it was just that she made him feel brave.

The confidence he felt, the confidence they all felt, kept them in place. It kept them hidden. It kept them safe. The thunder of the marching dissipated as the soldiers passed them.

Dec smiled. "Get a load of that. We just beat every stormtrooper in this place and we didn't have to throw a single punch."

"Some fight." Lorica rolled her eyes.

"Counts," Dec said. "A million stormtroopers— zero. J-Squadron—one."

He gave Mattis and Sari a wink and a grin before taking off again. Lorica just took off again.

Sari had that look once more.

"I don't remember meeting Dec, and he doesn't remember meeting me. I probably met AG first. That seems to be their way, doesn't it?"

That had been the case with Mattis, though he vividly remembered meeting Dec. He was pure mischief from the start but also, no matter how much it may have seemed otherwise, a true friend.

"We'd seen each other around. We hadn't known each other, then we kind of did. He told me about Ques and asked me about my home, and talking about it stung, so I stopped."

Sari looked past Mattis and nodded. Mattis turned to see Lorica was waving them on again. Dec was with her this time. Mattis could see that Dec was upset about something from the agitated way he was talking.

"Let's go," Sari said, tapping Mattis's chest with the back of her hand.

They sprinted across an exposed hallway to a recess in the wall on the periphery of the base.

Mattis could feel the chill of the wind whipping around. Snow drifted in and melted on his skin. Dec looked interrupted by their arrival. He almost seemed embarrassed.

"I'm sure it's fine," Lorica told him.

"I reckon we'll hash it out on our way off this rock," Dec said.

Lorica gave Dec the kind of look that Mattis was used to. It was a look she shot him when he realized something she'd been trying to explain for ages.

Dec didn't give them a smile this time as he ran ahead.

"What was that about?" Mattis asked Lorica.

"Nothing. We're almost there. Wait for my signal."

Lorica sprinted away.

Mattis looked at Sari expectantly. "Tell me the rest of what you were saying. We have to wait for them anyway."

"So," Sari continued, picking up where she'd left off, "I needed to resolve my homesickness. I gave myself until the end of the week to decide whether to stay with the Resistance or go back home. The night before my deadline, I went to my bunk. There, resting on my pillow, was something that would make my decision for me."

Mattis's mind raced. He imagined a little Jedi Master lying on her pillow, dispensing wisdom or prophesy.

"It was a box," she said.

"Oh." Mattis was a little disappointed.

"It looked like a boot case, but the edges were rounded off. I opened it, and I was hit with familiar smells before I could even see inside. Ertelberries! Silverio tea! Stormfruit candies made by hand! A haul of my favorite spices from the Harvest, everything from Ditkoff hottercorns to Doctor Ryross's grilled salt. Baraan-Fa was with me on D'Qar."

"Wow!" exclaimed Mattis. The Jedi Master had sent her a care package! Then he remembered there was not necessarily a Jedi Master in this story.

"There was no card, no letter. No return address. Nobody back home knew where I was. I wondered who could have possibly sent it. Then I spied Dec and AG in the far doorway. Dec gave a little wave, and then they went off, laughing at some shared joke like they do. I don't know how they'd figured out my favorite things from home, much less how they got them to D'Qar so quickly, but I knew they had done it. My decision was made. I got in that bed and curled up, which I had never done before. It's not how I sleep, but you know what?"

"You fit?" Mattis guessed.

"I fit." Sari nodded. "I slept soundly that night. And for the next month, I put hottercorns on every meal."

Sari looked Mattis in the eye. He only just realized because of it that she hadn't been looking at him for most of the story. She'd been looking all around. Anywhere but in his eyes. Whatever she was about to tell him, he felt it was the crucial part it had all been leading up to. He wasn't wrong.

"I've always loved Dec. But I never *liked* him before," she said, stressing the word *liked* to mean something that outstripped and sidestepped both *like* and *love*. "I just want to be clear. I said it's a crush, but . . . it isn't. He means something to me."

"That's great!" He beamed. "At least potentially! I've been keeping it a secret, but I like someone, too."

Sari nodded as if she already knew what Mattis was telling her, but there was no way she could have. Sari was smart, so the way she nodded was sometimes as though she already knew stuff. That was probably the case now, Mattis thought.

"Do you think he likes you back?" Mattis asked.

"Dec wears his emotions like a Life Day sweater." Sari shook her head. "If he liked me back, I'd know it."

She kicked a little rock. It skittered a short distance into the wilderness surrounding the base.

"Dec and I have talked about everything under every sun together, and I've never known him to like a girl. It's just not how he is." She bit her lip. "I'll have to figure out what to do with my feelings. Luckily, if there's one thing I'm wired for, it's figuring things out."

She suddenly wore a puzzled expression and crouched down to look at the rock she had kicked.

"That's strange," she murmured. "How could you possibly have a shadow like that?"

She took a step closer to it and then looked into the sky, transfixed. Mattis followed her outside the base and into the wild. He looked up and was just as struck.

The sun looked . . . wrong. Mattis couldn't figure out what he was looking at. It was as if the planet were drinking the sun through a straw! There wasn't a straw, though. Was it a tractor beam? How would that even work? Mattis remembered from his time on Vodran what it was like to feel crazy, because at that moment, looking at a thing that couldn't and shouldn't have been able to be, he felt perfectly and completely bonkers.

"What in the Force is that?" he asked.

"This planet is draining its sun," Sari said. "But to what end? Why would anyone need that much solar energy?"

It took her as long to come up with the answer as it had to think of the question. "They're powering their weapon. They'll be able to destroy tens of planets in a single go!"

"That's amazing!" Mattis was in awe. "Your brain."

"If only I were able to process my emotions as quickly."

Mattis's eyes started to complain from looking at the sun.

"At least you know what's going on in Dec's mind. I never know what the person I like is thinking," Mattis said, rubbing his eyelids with his palms to squeeze the blur spots out. When he opened his eyes, Lorica was standing in front of them, fuming.

"Sari," Lorica started. "Mattis," she continued, trying and failing to contain her annoyance. "I need you," she said slowly and deliberately, "to focus on the mission. The mission, as you know, is important. It's life or death."

Sari and Mattis mumbled apologies and agreement to focus on the mission. Lorica wasn't done.

"Emotions are supposed to work for you, not the other way around! That's what they teach us day one, minute one in Zeltron grade school. Everyone on this mission is being led around by their stupid emotions!"

"They're not stupid," Mattis protested.

"That right there," Lorica said, pointing to

Mattis's head, "is where smart lives. And that"—she gestured dismissively at the rest of him—"is where emotions live. Unless, of course, you're a Zeltron. We keep all of our emotions up here"—she tapped her temple—"and all of yours, too. Which gets in the way of thinking and focusing and, most importantly, the mission!"

"Which emotions are Dec feeling that are interfering with the mission?" Sari asked, hope embroidered around the edges of the question.

"Not what you think. He's worried about his last exchange with AG. Thinks AG might be glitching and not know it. Dec's trying to stay on mission, but he keeps worrying for his kin. But the thing that you do think about Dec? That's a good instinct."

"Did you hear us?" Mattis asked, worried that he might have said something he desperately didn't want her to hear and also, just as desperately, *did* want her to hear.

"No," Lorica snapped, her annoyance giving way to irritation. "I can hear your feelings yelling themselves straight into my brain! Honestly, the odds of success of this mission, as with every

J-Squadron mission, would be astronomically higher if it were a solo mission!"

"Anger is an emotion," Mattis said.

Sari stifled a snicker.

"That wasn't anger. It was irritation becoming frustration! This is anger, Mattis! This! This right here is anger!"

"Then pull it together, Demaris," Mattis said calmly. "We're on a mission, and we can't have emotions get in the way of that."

Sari let out the snicker this time. Lorica fumed, then stopped. She led Mattis and Sari quickly and quietly through the last of the base, where many of the First Order military were quartered. It was slightly less oppressive, as the grid of living spaces didn't go up into the sky so much as sprawl out some distance. Mattis experienced a slightly strange feeling that he realized was his eyes adjusting to the natural light overhead. Without towering structures around, this area felt exposed, though he was certain it was well-observed and protected.

Dec was posted in a corridor a stone's throw from their destination. He held up a hand as

Lorica, Mattis, and Sari reached him. In training, they'd learned some hand signals for silent communication. At the time, Dec seemed incapable of paying attention, much less ever learning the signals, and yet he demonstrated perfect recall. He indicated that eleven stormtroopers stood between them and the Jerjerrod's quarters, a front-facing unit. Dec established their positions and their weapons.

Dec and Lorica went back and forth with different hand signals, offering plans of attack. Sari measured each one and shook her head no again and again. The quick hand movements reminded Mattis of wheat/stone/river, a game they had played at the orphan farm. Mattis was a master of wheat/stone/river. He won a tournament once. He'd kept the ribbon until he lost it. It made him feel a little sad to realize that the odds were great he would never see that ribbon again. He realized he was getting distracted, and that was when inspiration struck!

Mattis placed his hands together at the pointer fingers and thumbs, and he made a scratching motion with his pinkies. Nobody saw. They were watching each other. Mattis pushed his hands into the middle of the four of them and scratched at the air with his pinkies again, jaggedly, thinking the word that it meant as loud as he could think, imagining he was yelling *distraction* with his fingers.

They all agreed that they could use a distraction. That wasn't a whole plan, but enough of one that would make everything easier. But what distraction could they create?

Mattis gritted his teeth and summoned the Force. He felt his neck go tight. He gestured as hard as he could at the Jerjerrod quarters. He pulled at the air around his hands, insisting with his will that the roof would peel off and it would come down hard on a tight group of stormtroopers. That would distract the rest of them for sure. He pulled so hard at the roof he thought his ears would pop or his nose would bleed. He closed his eyes and wished even harder for reality to do his bidding.

Mattis opened one eye to make sure Lorica was impressed by his efforts. She wasn't. He started to feel self-conscious about what he was doing. He nearly stopped, but Dec grabbed his right hand and gave an encouraging squeeze, as if to say, *If you can't do it alone, maybe we can do it together.*

Dec gritted his teeth as Mattis had done.

Sari took Mattis's left hand, held out her other hand, and furrowed her brow. Mattis felt a swell in his chest. Was it the Force?

It was the feeling of laughing late at night at something Klimo had said. It was the feeling of racing hover-bikes with AG. It was the feeling of Lorica smiling at him, which she was now doing.

The roof did not peel off.

In fact, nothing happened.

And then from above and from a distance, Mattis heard a familiar but not immediately recognizable sound. As it got louder and closer, Mattis hoped that he recognized it, because if he was right, it might be the most welcome sound he had ever heard.

He was right! A squadron of X-wings tore across the sky.

The Resistance had arrived! Mattis bet it was Black Squadron up in those ships. He imagined Poe Dameron leading Jess and Snap and the rest of them to victory. The X-wings rained laser fire on the base and circled around to do it again. It was all Mattis could do to keep from cheering. He looked to his friends and saw that they were just as excited as he was.

Not the Force, he thought, *but any distraction in a storm.*

Now the question was how to use it to their advantage. It appeared to have the opposite effect Mattis had hoped. The stormtroopers were on edge, more alert than they had been before. They had their blasters out of their holsters and at the ready. They seemed not only prepared to start blasting but eager to do it. The mission had just gotten more difficult.

Mattis nearly jumped out of his skin when a siren wailed long and loud. The stormtroopers ran off in formation to do, Mattis supposed, whatever stormtroopers did when an alarm went off.

There was nobody and nothing in the way of the Jerjerrods' quarters.

"You did it!" Dec slapped Mattis's cheek twice playfully.

Lorica shook her head.

"Let's just get Jo and get out of here," she huffed. "If he's even in there."

That stopped Mattis cold. Jo might not be in there! He hadn't thought of that. They all just assumed that's where he'd be. Where would they look if he wasn't in there? On a base like this, there definitely were interrogation chambers. Probably there were tons of them! Mattis had no doubt that the one where they were holding Jo was right where they came in, that they'd snuck their way around the base for nothing. That was the way his luck ran.

"Hey," a harsh voice demanded behind them. "Who are you and what are you doing here?"

The voice belonged to a very blond, very perfect if cruelly composed woman in a copilot's uniform.

Yes, that was the way Mattis's luck ran. Not only wouldn't they rescue Jo, but they would need to rescue themselves.

Dec stood up straight and addressed the woman.

"We're the Hansens," he said, motioning at himself and Sari without missing a beat. "She's the Demaris girl," he pointed at Lorica, "and that's Mattis Banz."

Something about Dec's speech struck Mattis as strange. Dec was making a sour face and doing a crisp accent. But why?

"We live here on the base. Our parents all work here," Dec continued. "Do you know them? Tybee and Verona Hansen. They work on the AT-ATs. I don't know if I'm supposed to talk about that, actually. Forget I said anything. Diff Resto Demaris. Accounting. I think that's okay to say. Cowen Banz? I think he's a moff. Mattis, did your father make moff or did they pass him over again?"

Then it hit Mattis. Dec was pretending that they were all First Order progeny, so he was mimicking what that sounded like, as far as he knew. Dec was doing an impression of Jo! Mattis had to bite his lip not to laugh. It was a good impression. He didn't nail the accent, but the manner was perfect. He looked up at the copilot to see if she bought it. Mattis's urge to laugh fell away in the face of her scowl.

"He's a moff," Mattis said, looking up at the

copilot. She was huge. Mattis doubted Sari could even make a dent in her.

"Moff Banz. Do you know him?"

The copilot looked them over one by one. Mattis felt as though she knew they were lying and was deciding the best way to debone each of them. Where to start and what to do with all the bones.

"The base is under attack. Did you see those X-wings? Go to your quarters. Await instructions."

"Yes, ma'am." Dec saluted. "Come on, guys, let's go."

That was the last of their lucky breaks. Things turned bad quickly after that. Wanten came around the corner. He spotted his former prisoners and yelled, "Resistance! Resistance, deBoer! Stop them!"

The copilot drew her blaster, but Lorica kicked it from her hand. The copilot, deBoer, swung at Lorica, who parried the blow with her forearm. Lorica spun around, driving her other elbow into deBoer's abdomen. DeBoer then punched Lorica twice in the small of her back, and Lorica dropped. DeBoer came at her, but Lorica swept the copilot's legs out from under her. They got up slowly. They regarded each other like a Wookiee squaring off against a Trandoshan. This fight would take a while.

Dec hated whiles. He scrambled for the blaster.

Wanten made a run for the blaster too. Purely on instinct, Mattis got in his way. He put up his fists and bounced on the balls of his feet, prepared to trade blows, but Wanten had well over a hundred pounds and half a meter on Mattis. Surprisingly fast, Wanten grabbed Mattis. Mattis threw a fist and got Wanten good once, bloodying the man's pig nose. Wanten yelled a short vowel sound and spun Mattis around to put Mattis between himself and the blaster Dec now held. Wanten had one arm around Mattis's chest and the other around his throat. He squeezed slightly, and Mattis's head began to spin.

He could hear Wanten and Dec yelling at each other, but he couldn't make out just what they were saying. He could see that the fight continued between Lorica and deBoer. It was blurry. He felt as though he was missing an amazing battle. He could see Sari trying to figure out whom to help

and how. He wanted to tell her not to worry. It would all be fine. He felt as though he was about to go to sleep and that time was slowing down to accommodate everyone.

Then a TIE fighter fell out of the sky, crashed into the Jerjerrod quarters, and exploded.

CHAPTER

09

A LOT OF PEOPLE'S parents used counting as a tool to convince their children to quickly obey.

"You'd better clean your plate before I count to ten, young man."

Or "You have until the count of three to start brushing your teeth."

Jo had heard about parents like that. Count-to-ten fathers were everywhere. Jo had been in many count-to-three mothers' homes. Some parents alternated between ten-counts and three-counts. Some planets, Jo heard, were strictly count-to-five planets. To shorten to three or expand to ten would seem strange on a count-to-five planet.

Jul Jerjerrod only ever counted to one.

She was a wonderful, caring, attentive mother who did all the voices in every bedtime story she ever read. She was an accomplished pilot and high-ranking officer of the First Order. She had been born on a wild planet in the Outer Rim but carved out a life on Tinnel IV. She had fallen in love only twice. She adored books about history, and when she found a passage that was particularly compelling, she would read it aloud to her son no matter what else he was doing. Jo tended to be pleased both to hear something interesting and that his mother was so enthusiastic in her enjoyment of historical facts and her affection for him. He would listen attentively. She would do all the voices. Her Darth Vader impression was terrible.

She hardly ever disciplined her son. She hardly ever had to. He only wanted to make his parents proud. On the rare occasion that Jo's course needed correcting, Jul was impatient with that part of it. She wanted the educative or intimidating portion of their lives to be over so they could be united in purpose and sentiment once more.

So she would only give him to the count of one.

The count to one gained prominence in the Jerjerrod household after the Boddees moved away. It was a time of petulant moods. It was a time of slammed doors. It was a time of resentment, distrust, anger, and change.

"I'm going to count to one," his mother would say, and Jo had better have set the table or cleared it or started his homework or woken up or gone to bed.

It worked every single time.

Jul had proscribed against his letting her reach "one" on perhaps a dozen occasions, and on none of them had she ever reached the start and end of counting.

In his parents' quarters on Starkiller Base, as his mother held a blaster on him, Jo once more heard his mother say, "I'm going to count to one."

She informed him that he had better settle down and be ready to talk reasonably and civilly, but a lot had changed since the last time she had threatened to count to one.

"No," Jo said, as surprised as anyone in the quarters by that, much less by what followed. "*I'm*

going to count to one," he told her, "at which point you had better lower your weapon."

"No," Jul countered. "*I'm* going to count to one."

"I'm going to count to one," Jo said louder.

Jo's father tried to intercede. He held up his hands and looked back and forth between his wife and his son.

"Come on now," was as far as he got.

Jul stretched out her blaster arm as if citing it as the argument winner. "I'm going to count to one."

"Now let's—" Jax tried again.

"You don't count to one," Jo interrupted. "I count to one! And I'll do it. I'll count to one, and if you don't lower that blaster by the time I get to one, you'll be sorry."

"*You'll* be sorry," she said, "if I start counting and I get to one. *You'll* be sorry."

"That's it," Jo said. "I'm going to count to one."

"Don't you count to one. I'm counting to one," his mother told him, narrowing her eyes like she meant it.

"Nobody count to one," Jo's father commanded, but no one listened.

"I'm counting to one," Jo said.

"No, I'm—" his mother started to counter once more when she was interrupted by an alarm. She looked away, lowering her blaster and breaking their standoff. It should have felt like a win. Instead, it punctured Jo in a deep part of him that he was less commanding of his mother's attention than an anonymous First Order siren was.

She looked back at Jo, annoyed.

"Is this you?" she asked him. "This alarm. Is this because of you?"

"Me?" Jo couldn't believe it. "What? No!"

"Did you do something? What did you do?"

"What could I do? I've been a captive since before I got here!"

Her face scrunched up into a pucker as if she was trying to figure out if Jo was lying.

"Why don't you ask *him*?" Jo pointed at his father. "He's the one who does something."

"What did *I* do?" his father asked.

"I don't know, Dad," Jo erupted. "It's been years and I still don't know what you did! Najeema was my best friend!"

Jo tried to force his tears to stay inside. His throat tightened and he had to choke out the words. "His family was—" He tried to think of the word that summed them up. The word that mattered. "They were *kind*," he finished.

"Jo," his father said, and reached out.

"Don't." Jo recoiled. "They didn't just move away like you said," he spat. "You moved them. Or had them moved. Or worse."

Jo's father's face became impenetrable. It wouldn't answer the question Jo was asking any more than his father ever had.

"You," Jo's mother said to Jo, "do not talk to your father like that. The neighbors saw too much. They saw the plans for . . . well, you're standing on it."

Jo was stunned.

"It's war," she said coldly. "Your friend and his family were casualties."

Casualties. The word landed hard on Jo.

"No!" he screamed. "No!" He wanted to say so much, about hypocrisy and fairness and friendship and family and lies and horror and death and trust, but his thoughts were a firestorm and he couldn't pluck any individual ones to lay out. He felt ineloquent, sick, slapped, and lightheaded.

"Your father didn't do anything he wasn't ordered to do," Jo's mother said, looking around the quarters absentmindedly. "Ordered to do by me. I give the orders. It's called rank, thank you very much." She continued to look around.

Jo wished she'd at least pay attention to him as she broke his heart.

"Speaking of orders, you"—she handed Jo's father the blaster—"take this. That alarm is for me. I have a unit waiting. Have you seen my cap?"

"It's right there." Jax pointed to the credenza, where a military officer's cap lay neatly on a shelf.

She was reaching for it when the TIE fighter crashed through the ceiling and exploded.

CHAPTER
10

AG AWAITED THE SIGNAL to pick up the rest of J-Squadron. He and Ymmoss, Klimo, and Cost had gained entry to the hangar and stolen past rows of immaculate TIE fighters to find a ship the right size. He drummed his fingers on the armrest of the captain's seat of a First Order light shuttle. His metal digits plunked satisfyingly against the thick leather of the armrest. AG was excited to pilot this ship. It was sleek and mighty. It would handle well; he could tell it would fly smooth and make him look good. He had nothing against this ship. It was fast and strong and, most important, big enough for all of J-Squadron to fit. He liked this ship. It was the right ship for the job.

But AG was dying to pilot a TIE fighter! AG doubted there was a more responsive ship in the galaxy. TIE fighters were so compact! So elegantly designed! His dream was to fly an X-wing someday, sure. His nightmare, however, was to be reprogrammed to fight for the bad guys and fly a TIE fighter. The wicked thrill he got from a nightmare about flying a TIE fighter was the best part of a bad dream. He meant to, in the course of such nightmares, dream of un-reprogramming himself and switching sides to fight for the Resistance again in his brand-new TIE fighter. Whenever he had those nightmares, though, he would inevitably forget to care about his pro-gramming in favor of just flying.

But this light shuttle was a good machine. It was of requisite size, unlike those hundreds of exhilarating TIE fighters all around. One-seaters. No, thank you.

AG reviewed the maps for the base and plot-ted several courses of escape. He remembered to spend a little effort on being mad at Dec, now that he wasn't too busy.

Ymmoss let out a little purr. AG hadn't noticed, but as he idly cycled through maps and anger in his head, he had started petting his copilot. He was giving her a good skritching. All pilots with furry seconds must have done this from time to time, AG figured. He suspected he might have been just holding out his hand and Ymmoss found it, put the back of her head under it, and let instinct take over. Regardless, she'd earned it.

AG turned a little to see what Cost and Klimo were up to. Klimo was teaching Cost to sit in a chair and do her own strapping in. The results were fair, but they had time to improve, AG thought. Cost had wrapped up her leg in an arm strap somehow. Klimo tried to have her start over when his antenna started twitching. He went still and motioned for Cost to stop wriggling, as well.

Seconds later, an alarm went off.

AG stopped scratching Ymmoss and looked to the display. She leaped up and inspected Klimo and Cost, who remained frozen and accepted inspection.

"I don't think it's the ship making noise," AG said. "Nothing's lit on the dash."

Ymmoss purred agreement. Still, she moved

Klimo and Cost to peer around them for any buttons or levers or other potential ways they might be responsible. She shrugged. There was nothing there.

"If it's not us," Klimo said, "how can we turn it off?"

"Wee-oop!" Cost yelled, echoing the alarm. "Wee-oop, wee-oop, wee-oop!" She started a countermelody, accompanying the alarm as if they were singing a song together.

"Hey, neat!" Klimo exclaimed. He started clapping a rhythm and finding a serviceable harmony.

As AG lowered himself off the chair to the floor, he remembered that Klimo once told him he came from a musical family. He pointed out to Ymmoss that stormtroopers were filing into the hangar. She ducked down out of sight, as well. No reason to panic Klimo and Cost, AG thought as they continued making up their song. They were small, and their chairs were big. They were unlikely to be seen from outside. Alerting those two would likely put all of them in worse danger. *A crack team I'm leading here,* AG thought.

When TIE fighters started lifting off all around

them, it was harder to hide from Klimo what was happening. It was the same amount of difficulty to keep Cost from noticing. The Rodian boy saw the ships go and stopped his singing. He nodded to AG on the ground and slid slowly down his own chair toward the floor. Klimo's shirt dragged on the edge of the chair and rode up, exposing his bumpy, pickle-green belly. Once he was safely on the floor, he tried to fix his shirt, but it was a hard thing to do while horizontal. It kept him busy and distracted, at least. He tried marching across the floor on his shoulder blades and elbows to get his shirt back on right. It was eventually successful, but then his pants had slipped too low on his narrow waist, exposing remarkably clean underpants. AG and Ymmoss watched transfixed as Klimo flipped onto his stomach and wriggled backward to Cost's continuous and unabashed tune. Ymmoss blinked and was slightly surprised every time she opened her eyes and found the same show happening in front of her.

When the hangar was nearly empty of TIE fighters, the alarm stopped. That's when Cost finally noticed something.

"What happened to my song?" she asked.

AG glared at the comm, wishing Dec's signal would come while every TIE fighter was distracted and nobody was interested in their ship. *It would be a good time for a signal*, he thought at the comm. *A perfect time.* AG added this small frustration to Dec's tab, despite the fact it wasn't in any way Dec's fault.

The floor underneath AG started vibrating. The aft hatch was opening. Before AG had a chance to even process it, Ymmoss was up and pouncing toward the rear of the ship. She reached through the hatch as it opened and grabbed an unsuspecting stormtrooper waiting to board. She pulled him into the door so hard his helmet couldn't protect him. It all happened so quickly that seven of the eight remaining stormtroopers were completely stunned. The eighth stormtrooper pulled his blaster and aimed it at the hatch. He didn't have a chance to get off a shot before Ymmoss threw the first stormtrooper at him.

AG felt a pang of guilt in that moment. He knew Dec would have wanted to see that.

Ymmoss roared at the seven remaining stormtroopers. Then Klimo did. He sprang up, roared again, charged, ran up Ymmoss's back, and leaped

at the two closest stormtroopers, hooking their necks in his arms and taking them down to the ground. He pulled off one of their helmets and knocked its owner out with it before using it to crack the shell on the other one.

"I made it through exactly four hundred and twelve beasts, creatures, and monsters to find my friends again!" he yelled as he pulled the helmet off the second, now unconscious stormtrooper. "I had to get through seven of you black-and-white plastic-shelled jerk soldiers just to get a ship to follow my friends off that swamp planet!" Klimo whacked another stormtrooper's blaster out of his hands with one helmet and slammed the other helmet into his stomach, doubling him over. "You think you can stop me now that I'm *with* them? You cannot!" He swung the helmet at the stormtrooper's head, knocking him down and out. "I became a beast on that planet and now I'm a beast on this planet, too!" he yelled and roared.

Ymmoss roared again, too, and jumped in the fight. The two of them tore through the remaining stormtroopers in a ballet of violence.

"I'm not much for scrappin'," AG said to no

one in particular. He hadn't budged from the captain's chair. "Let us know if you need us though, right, Cost?"

Cost struggled to get loose of her straps, then rushed into the fray, flailing her arms and yelling "I'll save you!"

AG hoped she wasn't talking to the storm-troopers.

CHAPTER

11

I T WAS CHAOS. The bad kind.

Mattis's ears rang like a shrill wind that wouldn't stop. He tried to focus, not that it mattered. All he could see was smoke. The good news was that he could mostly breathe; the smoke wasn't helping, but he wasn't being choked anymore. He resolved to avoid that sensation in the future at any cost. His chest was sore, as if he'd been punched by a droid. A piece of the building or the TIE fighter must have hit him. He was on his back on the ground. He turned his head carefully, as if he might scramble something or tip a piece of his brain out if he moved too quickly.

Wanten was laid out nearby, eyes closed, a patch of blood on his temple. Two stormtroopers tended to Wanten, and that's when Mattis noticed there was a stormtrooper kneeling above him, too.

"You with me, kid?" he heard the stormtrooper ask over the whistling.

The stormtrooper spoke loudly, as if it wasn't the first time he'd asked the question.

Mattis started to nod, then looked past the stormtrooper. He saw X-wings chasing TIE fighters in the sky. He gave a woozy wave to the Resistance ships.

The stormtrooper held up three fingers. Did Mattis think he was waving at him? He wasn't. Was that how stormtroopers waved? What a dumb way to wave. *Why is he doing that?* thought Mattis. He was grumpy and headachy.

"How many fingers am I holding—*AARGH!*" The stormtrooper keeled over onto Mattis's legs, his chest plate smoldering.

He'd been blasted. Through the clearing smoke, Mattis saw Dec running and blasting at stormtroopers. They were everywhere! Some attended to injured officers who must have been in nearby quarters hit by the explosion. Some sifted through rubble. Three stormtroopers were creeping up on Dec where he had stopped to clear a jam in his blaster. Before Mattis could cry out in warning, Lorica leaped out and clobbered one of the stormtroopers with a pair of stun batons. She sent the second to his knees as the third reached for his blaster. She strode forward between them, sending one baton down into the kneeling stormtrooper's helmet and the other up into the chin of the one who'd pulled a gun. She spun on her heel and finished the last stormtrooper with both batons. Mattis had just started to wonder what happened to Lorica's adversary, that copilot deBoer, when deBoer tackled Lorica into a residence building whose exterior wall had been collapsed by the TIE fighter wing that leaned against the back wall.

I should help her, Mattis thought. He tried to pull himself out from under the stormtrooper lying across his legs, which sent a ripple of ache across his whole body. He looked back to see Lorica knock deBoer out of the room. He wouldn't be much help to her or anyone until he was free. He was trying to kick off the stormtrooper when a stray shot from the battle in the sky landed near Mattis's hip. Debris hit his left pinkie knuckle hard, but he was glad to hear the rat-a-tat of more debris against the stormtrooper's armor over the receding high-pitched frequency.

He could hear alarms sounding sporadically, like a drill. The electricity of a live wire buzzed somewhere nearby. Stormtroopers yelled orders at each other and tried to contain the scene. He heard his name, but it sounded both small and far away. It came from the direction of the newly destroyed Jerjerrod quarters. A large piece of furniture that looked to Mattis like a bookcase was lying almost flat; someone was pinned beneath it. Not just someone. It was Jo! Jo was alive! They'd found him! Mattis kicked himself free of the stormtrooper.

There was an older man also pinned underneath the furniture. That must be Jo's father. They looked enough alike, once you wiped away some of the blood on Jo's face, which Mattis did. He tugged at the bookshelf with all his might. He budged it not at all.

He stopped pulling, took a deep breath, thought about the Force, and tried again. It moved! Mattis felt vindicated but realized it wasn't the time to dwell on that. He imagined high-fiving the Force though, and thought, *Finally*.

It was, in fact, Sari and not the Force who moved the bookshelf. Her sleeves were shredded; she had scrapes and bruises up and down her arms. Mattis had always thought Sari's strength came from size and leverage, but her shredded shirt proved him wrong as her huge muscles bulged to lift the piece of furniture.

Jo rolled out from underneath with a groan and then pulled his father free.

"You can let go of the armoire, Mattis," Sari told him.

"*Armoire!*" Mattis exclaimed, letting it go so his fingers wouldn't get pinched under it. "That's some kind of bookshelf, right?"

Jo gave Mattis a withering look, but he couldn't maintain it. It turned quickly into a smile. "You don't know anything," he told Mattis. "I'm glad to see you though."

"I'm sorry," Mattis said. "I have this whistling

in my ears. It sounded like you said you're glad to see me." Mattis couldn't stop smiling.

Jo clapped a hand on Mattis's shoulder, which was as close to hugging as he ever got. "I was obviously talking to Sari," he said, grinning, as well. "Thanks for the rescue. It's a bit . . . overblown though, isn't it?" He motioned at the sky battle that was visible through the blasted wall, the stormtroopers, the fights going on all around them.

"We go all out for our friends," Mattis told him.

"Is that Dec?" he asked.

"Do you know these people?" a woman yelled. "Are they in your Resistance? Is that the Resistance up there?" She extended her thumb. "It is, isn't it? Is this you after all? Did you do this? I can't believe it. You did this! All of this! What did you do?"

"Mother," Jo sighed. "How could I have done this? I was your captive when all of this started."

Mattis thought Jo's mother was impressive, and not only because she showed no signs of having just been in close proximity to an explosion, not even a smudge on her uniform.

"Where's Lorica?" Jo asked. "Is she here? And AG?"

"Good to know you care for my brother after all," Dec called as he blasted a stormtrooper, adding, "Lorica's over there!"

Through the smoke, Mattis saw Lorica pinning deBoer with her batons against the windowless, wingless remains of the wrecked TIE fighter's carapace. Lorica smiled the smallest smile when she saw Jo. Jo nodded to her and returned the almost smile. *This is as good as it gets with these two,* Mattis thought.

DeBoer punched Lorica right in her small smile, sending Lorica stumbling back into a pair of stormtroopers. One stormtrooper grabbed Lorica's batons, and the other took hold of her arm.

Too close for comfort, TIE fighters dogged X-wings just above them. They all paused to watch the aerial combat. An X-wing raced after a TIE fighter, blasting away. A piece from the wing of the TIE spun off faster than anyone could follow into the stormtrooper who had taken Lorica's batons, cleaving him in two! In one swift move,

Lorica plucked one baton from the air and used it on the stormtrooper who had grabbed her arm. He was on the ground in a moment.

Lorica turned back to deBoer, who held Lorica's other baton. DeBoer fired up its charge. Lorica did the same.

"First Officer deBoer," Jo's mother said. "Our battle is up there."

"Yes, ma'am," deBoer said, backing away slowly, powering down the baton, and keeping her eyes on Lorica.

Lorica advanced like a predator on her adversary. But then a phalanx of stormtroopers jogged briskly between them, flanking a high-ranking, ginger-haired officer with a disposition of disgusted military disappointment.

"General Hux, are you leaving us?" Jo's mom asked.

"Yes, well, as you can see," he gestured around him to indicate the chaos, "there's all of this. As much as I long to stop and chat, I shall do neither. Had I the time to wish you a good day, I assure you I would."

"Perhaps instead of time, you might spare

some of those troops to help us with"—she gestured—"all of this."

"Yes, fine, whatever. You." He indicated a section of his escort. "Do as she says. The rest of you, with me!"

He left, raising his collar as if it would protect him from anyone engaging him in further conversation.

"Those three and that one and there's one more," Jo's mother told the twenty stormtroopers at her disposal, pointing to Mattis, Jo, Lorica, Dec, and Sari. "They're with the Resistance. Apprehend them with alacrity, please. I'm due in the air. Overdue, really."

"Jul, I have this," Jo's dad said. "Honestly. Go."

She looked him over, licked her thumb, and wiped soot off his chin. She scanned the ground and found what she was looking for. A blaster. She handed it to her husband. He kissed her cheek. She gave him an expectant look.

"Collect the Resistance members," he told the stormtroopers. "Bring them to the interrogation rooms."

Jo's mom seemed satisfied. She turned to go.

DeBoer slid the baton into her belt and followed.

A stormtrooper fired up the crackling blue blades of a laser ax and told Jo to get down on the ground and interlace his fingers behind his head. He angled his weapon menacingly at Jo's chin. Lorica swung a baton at that stormtrooper's head so hard his helmet cracked. She took the laser ax and threw the baton to Jo, and never mind the odds.

"Forget this," a stormtrooper muttered, and drew his blaster.

"No! No guns!" Jo's dad yelled. "They're to be brought in alive. Unharmed. Not even stunned, do you hear me? Merely restrained."

"Not even stunned," Lorica taunted the holstering stormtrooper.

Jo barked out a laugh and added, "In fact, not even brought in."

"Not even that," Lorica agreed. "This is going to be fun."

Jo and Lorica had trained so extensively with weapons similar to the ones they currently wielded that Mattis couldn't blame them for showing off a little. He doubted that anyone but J-Squadron would notice, but Jo and Lorica took turns batter-ing the stormtroopers using similar maneuvers. Jo would act out a pattern of violence—head, back of the knee, chest, spin around, and get the head again. Then Lorica would do the same, but add another touch. Head, spin to get the back of the knee, chest, spin for the head. Jo followed that routine with a double spin at the end. Lorica gave him a little clap before leaping down onto the next stormtrooper, beginning a new sequence. Before long, they had taken down six stormtroopers without stopping to catch their breath. The stormtroopers, no longer as confident, encircled Lorica and Jo, who went back to back, daring their adversaries to come at them. Five stormtroopers took the dare and approached them brandishing large multisegmented spinning-ended riot con-trol batons. Jo and Lorica were no longer playful as they disarmed and dismantled their attackers.

Mattis saw Jo look past the stormtroopers. Was he distracted? Now? His mom hadn't left after all. She lagged behind and watched Jo fight. Mattis couldn't tell from her expression whether she was bothered or proud.

"I thought you were needed in the air!" Jo called. His mother shook her head and led deBoer away. Jo returned his focus to the fray.

There were still so many stormtroopers. Mattis worried for Jo and Lorica.

"Come on!" Sari snapped him out of his reverie, reminding Mattis that he was not merely a spectator but a part of this.

Sari put her head down and her shoulder forward and rammed her way into the circle. Sari scooped up two riot control batons from fallen troopers and tossed one to Mattis. It nearly knocked him over, and Mattis was struck once more by how strong Sari was. The two of them made their way to Jo and Lorica just as Dec did. He'd been blasting through from the other side. He also lugged a riot control baton. Jo looked down at his comparatively small stun baton.

"I want to get one of those big ones," he said. Everyone powered up their weapons. Jo and Lorica weren't the only ones who had participated in intense combat drills. As Mattis and his friends cut through the stormtroopers together, Mattis reflected on how much he loved that part of their training. He had not just loved it for the adrenaline rush of the fight, or just because he took to it reasonably well. He loved any sim or situation that put the members of J-Squadron together in pursuit of a common goal. J-Squadron got into trouble often, and while it might not have seemed so, there was no better place in the galaxy to be than watching the back of a fellow J-Squadron member, because they sure as the Force had yours. They delivered so much hurt to so many stormtroopers, Mattis wished Admiral Ackbar could have seen them. It was getting hard to maneuver with all the armored bodies at their feet.

"I have an idea and a blaster," Dec said. "The idea is to use the blaster to take out that commanding officer before he calls for more stormtroopers."

"No, Hansen," Jo said.

"The commanding officer is Jo's dad," Mattis whispered.

For perhaps the first time since they'd met, Dec didn't argue with Jo.

"What are you dumb idiots doing?" a familiar

terrible voice bellowed. "You're armed. Don't toy with them. Take them down!"

Wanten was conscious and on his feet again. He was still awful.

"Feel free to shoot *that* guy though," Jo said.

"I was about to," Dec replied, "but your pa got in the way."

Jo's dad talked quietly but heatedly to Wanten as Mattis whacked a stormtrooper into Dec's baton, which he slammed into the stormtrooper's stomach, throwing him into the air, where Sari swatted him with her enormous weapon.

"I don't care about any of that," Wanten windbagged. "It's nothing to me, do you hear me? Less than nothing. Less still than even that! Listen to me," he addressed the stormtroopers. "You were ordered to capture. You were ordered not to use lethal force. As the ranking officer on site, those orders are rescinded. I rescind them. They're rescinded! Use lethal force to incapacitate these Resistance scum. To death!"

"New plan," said Dec blasting the remaining stormtroopers on the far side of the downed TIE fighter. J-Squadron leaped into the shell of the ship for cover just as the shooting started.

"Dec," Lorica said. "Now would be a good time to signal AG."

"No kiddin'," Dec said, grinning. "I been signaling him since we first had visual confirmation on Jo." His smile gave way to real concern. "Where could he be?"

AG SAT ON the lip of the hatch, swinging his legs and blasting stormtroopers like he did long-necked snarlaps back home. Snarlaps were about the meanest nuisances. Just sour dispositions. They'd ruffle their feathers and come snapping. Back on Ques, AG and Dec would run them off for folks, and if they got extra helpings of dessert out of the deal, well that was A-okay. And if Dec got to eat AG's extras, that was fine by AG. Dec had been getting extra helpings—what they called "droid's portions"—since forever. AG wanted to add that to the pile of things about which he was angry with Dec, but really, AG didn't mind. He enjoyed shooting the snarlaps with Dec, and he liked blasting stormtroopers with J-Squadron now. Between the ones that had taken off in the TIE fighters, leaving exactly no ships for AG to fantasize about flying, and the ones who had come for the light shuttle and the ones who had come because they heard that J-Squadron had taken out their friends, the base must be running out of stormtroopers.

Klimo and Ymmoss fought side by side. It was a good team-building exercise, AG thought. Klimo had been so standoffish with Ymmoss at first. They had saved each other a few times now and cheered each other's occasional particularly stylish dispatch of a stormtrooper. AG was glad they had leaped into the fray, roaring and punching together. Now they were blasting away mostly but still occasionally going manual.

Cost wasn't much of a fighter. She drew everyone's attention from time to time with her volume and her frenetic activity. She was a wild card who kept the fight from growing too conventional. She was currently holding Ymmoss tight, like a baby partupi clinging to its mother as she slid along a tree branch looking for food. Cost punctuated the fight with taunting.

"How's that floor taste?" she asked an unconscious stormtrooper. "Ha! You thought I was a decorative hood, but I'm not, at least as far as I know!"

AG laughed at that. Cost would make a terrible pest of a hood, for one, and that stormtrooper could neither taste the floor nor make a judgment about what Cost was or wasn't.

AG shot a few blasters out of the hands of some newly arriving stormtroopers. He always liked blasting blasters. On realizing that about himself, he wondered if maybe he wasn't as odd as Cost in his own way. He liked her more in that moment because of how he reminded himself of her, or perhaps it was that she reminded him of him.

"Hang on, hang on!" AG yelled. He thought he heard something. "Everyone quiet down. Stop fighting for a second!"

The stormtroopers looked as if they were questioning whether this sort of thing was allowed. AG suspected that they were used to a voice of authority dictating their actions, and he did have authority in his voice.

It was quiet enough for AG to confirm that he had indeed heard something. His communicator was beeping out the signal.

"All right, wrap it up," he said to Ymmoss and Klimo. "We're needed."

Ymmoss gave him a look that said, *There are still a lot of these guys.*

"Fine. I'll help," AG said. He leaped out of the ship, grabbed a pair of fresh blasters, and raised them at the stormtroopers.

CHAPTER

13

L ASER FIRE PINGED against the TIE fighter. The shell of the ship wasn't going to pro- tect them for much longer, but that hardly seemed to matter now that the ground itself was cracking open. The whole planet seemed to shake, and then, ten meters away, it split with a baleful sound like a rancor that had lost its minder. The fissure sprang from the corridor they'd used to get there. It traveled in a path directly toward them like an accusing finger. It ran a meter long and five meters deep. The world groaned as one side of the hole sunk. Mattis could see the topmost stratum of soil under the constructed elements of the base.

"What's this now?" asked Dec.

"I think I know," said Mattis. "This planet is a Death Star, right?"

Sari explained the subtle differences between Starkiller Base and a Death Star, but it made no difference to Mattis.

"Whatever you call it, it's a murder planet. A giant First Order space weapon. The Resistance is coming for it like the rebels came for the Death Stars," he said, pointing to the sky fight. "This"— he made a circle with his finger, indicating the shaking planet—"is probably what happens if you're on the ground before the planet . . ." He trailed off because he didn't want to say the word *explodes* about a planet they were currently on.

"As for the extraction we're waiting for, should we assume the worst?" Jo asked.

"What would that be?" Dec challenged, his face only centimeters away, as they were all huddled inside a ship built to seat only one.

Jo stuck a blaster through an opening and shot it a few times. He'd taken a blaster from a felled stormtrooper; there were plenty to go around. J-Squadron were all armed with blasters now and had been able to keep the remaining storm-troopers from advancing, though they couldn't decrease the enemy's number in a significant way. Jo's blast kept the stormtroopers from getting close enough to get a good shot at J-Squadron.

"Should we assume that AG wasn't successful in his mission and that we need to find ourselves a ride off of this planet before it . . . ?"

He didn't trail off to avoid saying *explodes*. He trailed off because the crack that had started ten meters away from them wasn't done yet. The thin fracture grew like a midday shadow and headed toward them.

"No, Jo," Dec chafed. "We don't need a plan B."

"It would be better to have one and not need it than to need one and not have it."

"Is that an old Gungan expression?" Dec challenged. "Because it sure sounds like one."

"It sounds better in Gungan," Jo snapped back.

"There's no way that's true," Dec said. "Anyway, we don't need a plan B, and we won't. AG's got us."

"Dec," Sari said softly.

"Not you, too, Sari."

"We know how you feel about AG, but what if Jo's right?"

"He ain't right. You ain't right, Jerjerrod, so stop looking at me like I'm bein' a baby. It ain't about how I feel about my brother. It's about how that crack ain't all that's coming for us. Look up there." Dec pointed.

A light shuttle came down fast and hard, skidding meaningfully through what remained of the stormtroopers, flattening some and sending others flying. It was a thorough, completely intentional, prolonged skid performed with efficiency and style that didn't end until the last of the stormtroopers was dispatched. The hatch opened. There was Klimo, his arms in the air like a champion.

"Klimo!" Klimo yelled in celebration of being visible to his friends. He leaped from the shuttle and slid to a halt beside the TIE fighter they'd been using as protection.

The ground shook and carped as another crevice opened up right in front of the hatch. The crack from the alleyway split even deeper and farther, continuing toward J-Squadron.

"What's this now?" Klimo asked. "Is the planet going to explode like always happens when Death Stars get visited by rebels?"

Jo was stunned. "Klimo's alive? But how?"

"It's a long story," said Lorica.

"We assume it is," said Dec. "We haven't actually heard it. The shortest version is that he lived. Frankly, I don't need a long story from Klimo."

"The rancors had me. I was finished," Klimo began. "But then—"

Dec squeezed Klimo's snout shut. "What'd I just say?"

Klimo mumbled something between Dec's fingers.

"Tell you what," Dec said. "We live through this? Then I'll listen to your long story."

The ground shook again, cleaving and cracking all over.

"Hurry, friends," Klimo squeaked. The members of J-Squadron hurried for the shuttle. They leaped over growing crevasses and angry trenches that slashed the surface of the base.

Just as they reached the shuttle, a hulking figure stepped before its entry ramp. Wanten. He made a grab for Klimo, who yelped. Wanten dangled the scrawny Rodian a meter off the ground.

"No!" Mattis yelled. He raised his hands like an orchestra conductor and waved them to one side, a move that, if the Force were cooperating, would have sent Wanten into a nearby wall.

"Mattis." Lorica spun to look him in the eye. "You do not have the Force. You don't have it. Stop trying to use it. Stop seeing if you have it. Because you don't."

"You're so good at feeling everybody's feelings," Mattis said. "If I actually don't have the Force, why do I feel in my bones like I do?"

She sighed. "You don't, Mattis," she said. "You're going to hurt yourself or someone else. Please. Accept this." She touched his shoulder. Their eyes met. Hers watered as if she meant to cry, and Mattis could see that she was just trying to convey something important. She was trying to convey the truth.

Mattis slumped. His pinky knuckle throbbed. It hurt. Lorica's words hurt worse.

Wanten cleared his throat for their attention. "Hello!" he said in a singsong. He continued to dangle Klimo with one hand and in the other he held a thirty-year-old, Empire-issued blaster. It looked old, but Mattis had no doubt that it worked. "Hi! Remember me?" Wanten continued. "I have your little friend here?" Klimo squirmed and pleaded with his eyes to the rest of J-Squadron. "So, throw down all of your weapons. And you know, if you don't, then I'm going to blast your friend."

"That's not your blaster," Jo said. "That's my father's blaster. His father gave it to him. It was a gift from a stormtrooper commander."

"Well, for your information, I carried this sort of blaster when I was a stormtrooper. I'm very good with this kind of blaster. No one is better. But yes. This particular one is your father's. I relieved him of it, duty, command, and consciousness. Not in that order. Don't make me repeat myself or—"

"Fine," Jo said, throwing down his blasters.

Mattis dropped his blaster, too.

"I don't like this," Dec said, tossing down the blasters in his hands, then the three extra blasters he'd stuffed in his waistband. Lorica checked the safety, then tossed her blaster into the open crevasse to her right. Sari hadn't brought any weapons.

Another TIE fighter exploded in the air, raining dust and debris down on them. Smoke rolled around them. The ground shook again and didn't stop this time. Cracks spiderwebbed all around.

"Better hurry up and start shooting," Jo said, "or the ground will take us first."

"Yes, well," Wanten said, "when you're right, you're right."

He pointed the Jerjerrod family gun at Jo and said, "And when you're dead, you're dead."

Wanten squeezed his lips together in a tight smile. But before he could pull his trigger finger, a spinning gray riot control baton, fully charged and crackling with blue energy, hit him square in the face.

Jax Jerjerrod had hit Wanten so hard, Wanten dropped Klimo and flipped backward all the way around and then some. He landed flat on his belly.

Jax looked a mess. Black eye, bloody lip, singe marks all over. He limped when he took a step forward. He and Wanten must have gotten into it with weapons.

"Jo," his father said. "I need you to know this. I didn't kill the Boddees. I evacuated them secretly. Safely. I sent them back to their home planet."

"You disobeyed an order from Mother?" Jo asked. "But why?"

"He was—" His voice wavered, which produced an involuntary tear from Jo. "He was your friend. I couldn't do that to you."

The planet shook. More ground fell away.

Jax Jerjerrod steadied himself against Klimo's shuttle. "Go," he said. "Get out of here, Son, and don't ever come back."

"Father, come with us," Jo pleaded. "The planet isn't going to last much longer."

"Can you imagine?" His father tried to smile, but with his busted lip, he couldn't manage it. "Your mother would kill me."

They got on the ship. Jo waved good-bye to his father as the hatch closed.

Inside the ship, Jo looked from Cost to Ymmoss, who growled a greeting.

"You brought the whole prison with you," Jo

said. "Nice to see you guys. How did—" He stopped, flabbergasted by the sight of Dec grabbing AG with an intensity he'd never seen between them.

Dec pulled AG up out of the pilot seat.

"Hey!" AG yelled.

"You sore at me?" Dec asked.

AG nodded. He couldn't meet Dec's eye.

Dec shook his brother and yelled, "Tell me you didn't ignore my signal! Tell me you didn't put lives in danger!"

"Of course I didn't, Dec, and I'd be sorer to hear you even ask that if I wasn't so relieved y'all are alive!"

"Good," Dec said.

"Good is right," AG agreed.

"What did I even do to make you sore, so I never do it again?"

"It was that you were sore at me, just for a second, before you realized you were sore at the situation. I would honestly prefer that you never do it again, even for a second."

"It's a deal, Brother," he said, and pulled AG in for a hug.

The ground beneath the ship shuddered.

"All right." AG dropped into his seat. "Strap in, J-Squadron. Let's light this candle!"

AG turned the ship around to get space to take off. There, at what would be the end of their runway, stood Wanten. He pointed Jo's father's gun at them and yelled something they couldn't hear.

"That guy." AG shook his head. "When I pretended to be reprogrammed on Vodran and took orders from him, he was the worst. He hates droids so much. He blames us for ruining his career or something. Every word he said to me made my circuits crawl. He'd laugh to himself about what a lousy job I always did at everything, even though I did a perfect job every time. Every day, he'd tell me how much he detested droids and that if I wasn't perfect, he would scrap me at the end of the day. Every day he'd tell me I wasn't the droid he was looking for and that I better try harder the next day. I lived in fear every day that he'd shut me off. No way to live. I look at him and see everyone who tells me droids can't be pilots. Droids don't have brothers. Droids ain't people. And now he's trying to tell me I can't leave this sinking ship of a planet?"

AG revved the engine. The sound made Wanten realize that trying to block a ship, even a light shuttle, by standing in the way wasn't the best plan he'd ever had.

"Buddy, I'm the droid you've been looking for your whole danged life." AG gunned the engine and blasted off right through Wanten. Pieces of him slapped against the viewscreen.

"Whoops!" AG said with a smile in his voice. Chunks of Wanten flew off as they picked up speed.

Mattis, Jo, and Lorica looked behind them at Jo's father, growing smaller in the distance. He collected his family blaster from where it had landed. They watched him wipe it off on his shirt. They watched him run in the opposite direction until they couldn't see him anymore.

The ship jolted, and the three of them tumbled and fell.

"I said strap in," AG called. "There's still a firefight up here. I'm doing my best to keep us out of it, but no one is respecting that. An escape is no good if you break your necks during it, so buckle up and stay that way."

"Yeah, strap in," Cost told them, testing the connectivity of all the straps by dragging her finger along them. "If you need a teacher, ask Greeno for help."

"She means me," Klimo said, taking her hand in his. "Klimo," he told her.

Sari and Dec strapped in next to each other.

"Figure AG isn't the only one I need to jaw with," Dec said. "You been looking at me from a different angle all day. We also in a fight I don't know about?"

"No," said Sari. "I'm just going through something."

"You know any load you want to share is one I want to help carry."

"I do know that, thank you. I don't need anything from you. If there's one thing I'm good at, it's figuring stuff out. I just need time."

"Not very much time." Lorica leaned forward. "For how loud your emotions are, you're really aware, really healthy. You're doing everything you need to do. You're taking care of it."

"Thank you." Sari smiled, relieved.

Lorica leaned back.

"Is it okay that I don't know exactly what conversation we're having?" Dec asked.

"It's ideal," Sari said.

Ymmoss growled.

"I agree." AG nodded. "This is it. It's time to jump up through the battle zone and out the other side. Figure we're safe from First Order ships, as we're in a First Order ship ourselves. All we have to do is avoid the Resistance until we get far enough away from the fight to hail them, tell them it's us, and then we're home free."

"All we have to do," Dec said, "is maneuver through a firefight without anyone noticing."

"They're so busy shootin' at each other," said AG, "nobody will think of shootin' at us."

"It's not getting shot at that I'm worried about," Jo said. "It's the ships going as fast as they can everywhere all around. This ship is new to you! You know how well you'd have to maneuver in order to get through unscathed? Your skills would have to be amazing. Your reflexes would have to be insanely fast."

"You kiddin' me, Jo? I was built for this."

With that, AG-90 proved once and for all

that droids made excellent pilots. He maneu-
vered up and up, skirting between X-wings and
TIE fighters engaged in screaming combat. He
dodged laser fire without so much as singe-
ing the shuttle's chassis. Finally, he eased up on
the throttle and told them all to go look out the
portholes.

Dec whistled. The fight raged on below them.
AG had gotten them through.

"AG," Jo said, awed. "You may just be the finest pilot in the Resistance."

"He's better than that," Dec crowed. "He's the
best pilot there is."

"Uh-oh," AG said, worrying everyone. "We've
got a proximity alert. Now we're being hailed.
Get the weapons ready."

Lorica and Mattis looked over the weapons
consoles. Unlike the Hutt ship they'd taken what
seemed like ages before, this console was neatly
arrayed. Mattis equipped the laser cannons and
targeted the TIE fighter that chased them. He
nearly had it in his crosshairs when a familiar
voice came through the communicator.

"Attention, *Griffin*-class light shuttle, call sign

ten-E. What are you doing up here, Ten-E? This is a battlefield!"

"Stand down, Banz," Jo said, shocked. "You too, Demaris."

"What?" Lorica cried, ready for a fight. "Why?"

"Because I don't want you blasting my mother out of the sky," Jo said.

"Ten-E, please respond," Jo's mom commanded.

"What do I say?" AG asked.

"Jo," his mother said. "That had better not be you in there."

Jo unbuckled and grabbed the communicator.

"Why do you even care, Mother?" Jo asked. "Don't you have a war to fight?"

"Yes," she said. "Against you."

Jo looked physically struck by that.

"My whole life," Jo said, trying to maintain composure, "you've put the First Order over family. Just once, put your family first. Won't you do that? *Can* you?"

There was a long pause with only light static coming over the communicator. The TIE fighter that Jul Jerjerrod piloted stayed steady on their tail. Then, finally, after an interminable silence, the communicator crackled back to life. "Jothan Tiaan Jerjerrod! You are unauthorized to be in ten-E. You land that ship right now, I mean it." Jo's mother was going to sink them. Or blow them up maybe. Either way, it'd be bad for J-Squadron.

"Should I go to lightspeed?" AG asked.

"We'll lose the Resistance," Dec said. "We'll never find 'em again."

"She'll give us a warning," Jo said. "But it won't be much of one."

"Then what do we do?" Mattis asked.

"Don't make me shoot you down, young man. I will do it. I will shoot you and your friends out of the sky. Don't think I won't."

"Here we go," Jo said.

"You have to the count," she started, and Jo rolled his eyes, "of three."

"Three!" Jo exclaimed joyfully, as if a three-count was something to celebrate.

"Magic number, sure, but I don't see why we're so excited about it," Dec said.

"Three," Jo repeated, seemingly ecstatic, as if he'd gone around the bend.

"Three!" Cost yelled, having already gone around the bend.

"Why are we yelling about numbers?" Klimo yelled, too.

Jo shook his head. "Three. I can't believe it."

"That is not a lot of counting," Lorica pointed out.

"It's enough," Jo told them. Then, "AG, go. This is our chance. She's giving us a chance."

AG gunned the engine. The shuttle sped off through the clouds. Then, rather than fly higher and completely out of Starkiller Base's atmosphere, AG cut the ship down and back into the skirmish below. AG whipped the shuttle around an X-wing heading right at them, then turned the ship sideways to slide between two TIE fighters. The one on his tail never broke chase as AG took them back up above the fray again.

"Your ma is some pilot," AG said.

Jo nodded. "Finest I've ever seen."

"We need something to throw at her ship," Dec said. "But what?"

"Oh! Dec! I keep forgetting to tell you," AG said, perking up. "We had to fight for this ship, and Sari actually threw one stormtrooper at another stormtrooper! I kept meaning to tell you, but we kept being in the middle of something."

"I love that, AG, and way to go, Sari! I wish I could have seen it, but, Brother, we *are* in the middle of something right now!"

"Oh, are we?" AG asked.

A different voice came over the comms. This one was also familiar.

"We got your signal, Ten-E, and we're here for you. Sorry it took us a second. We had our hands full."

It was Poe Dameron! Mattis all but leaped out of his chair cheering he was so excited to see Poe's X-wing flanked by Snap Wexley's and Jess Pava's! AG flew their ship around behind the X-wings. Cost and Klimo stayed strapped in for safety. Jo, Dec, Sari, and Lorica watched from the window to see what the outgunned TIE fighter would do.

"Turn around," Jo whispered, his eyes closed, his body tense. "Please turn around."

Mattis put a hand on Jo's shoulder. Beyond Jo, through the porthole, Mattis saw Jul Jerjerrod's TIE fighter drop out of view then rise up again and fly the opposite direction. Away from the Resistance and away from Starkiller Base.

"She's doing it," Mattis said. "She's going. We're safe now, and so is your mom."

They were all relieved to see the TIE fighter recede.

"Thanks for the assist there, Snap," AG said. "How's it going down below?"

"Fight's over," Snap said. "We won. Take a look."

The Corellian freighter tore past them, its fall-apart façade giving lie to its amazing speed. Mattis and Sari beamed at each other, ecstatic in the knowledge that it must be the famous ship they'd heard about for years. In its wake, Starkiller Base was flaring up. There were small explosions all over the surface of the planet.

All color drained from Jo's face as Starkiller Base exploded. Lorica let out a soft sound and doubled over in pain.

"Lorica? What happened?" Dec asked her.

"She must be feeling Jo's emotions." Sari measured Lorica and Jo's identical expressions.

"My father was down there," Jo said in a small voice.

"You don't know that," Sari said. "Maybe he found a way off the planet."

"No way," Jo said. "They weren't ordering an evacuation, so he wouldn't have evacuated. It's that simple."

"He defied your mom's orders once," Mattis offered. "He might have evacuated. It's possible!"

"He defied my mother's orders to keep from hurting me," Jo said.

Mattis indicated Lorica, who was still reeling, and said, "Look how much it would hurt you if he—" Mattis stopped short of saying *died*. "Your dad would know that. He wouldn't put you through that pain."

"It's not the same," Jo said. "He just wouldn't evacuate. Unless they ordered it, he wouldn't leave. He just wouldn't."

Jo was stony and numb, but Lorica wailed and sobbed. Cost started crying, too. Klimo patted her shoulder and snorted back his own sympathetic grief.

"Jo, when I said maybe your father is okay"— Mattis looked over his shoulders as if he was about to tell a secret—"I was trying to be discreet. I have what's called 'the Force,' and it's a connection between everything in the universe. With my mind and my heart, I'm touching everything. I'm doing it right now. I can feel it, just as clear as Lorica can feel your heart. The Force tells me that your father got off the planet. He's out there. You'll see him again one day."

Lorica sniffled and stopped crying. Jo blinked for the first time since Starkiller Base exploded.

"Really?" Jo asked.

Mattis nodded.

"Thanks, Banz."

Lorica threw her arms around Mattis and hugged him, and Mattis's head swam. She let go and his head still swam.

"It's a nice thing you did. Telling Jo that about his dad." She spoke quietly so the others wouldn't hear.

"When has hope ever hurt anyone? It might even be true, you know?"

"So you accept it then, huh? That you don't have the Force?"

Mattis had spent his whole life assuming he had the Force. That he was the wielder of a special power that balanced light and dark. That he was connected with every living thing in the galaxy. Even as he'd told Jo that he could feel that his father was alive, Mattis knew he was lying. But it was a good lie. It was a lie to give hope to a friend. "I don't have the Force," Mattis admitted. "I have something better."

"Do not say 'friends,'" Lorica warned him. "Do not be such a sap, Mattis Banz."

"Friends," Mattis finished anyway. He knew it didn't make him a sap. He could tell from her smile that she didn't really think he was one. He realized that it was enough for him. Whether she liked him back or not, they'd always be friends. They all would. Mattis leaned back in his seat and beamed at his squad. Klimo pointed out familiar parts of space to Cost, who said hello to each part. Jo and Dec recounted their stormtrooper battle for AG and Ymmoss, each one highlighting the great moments of the other. Sari laid on a long bench seat and napped quietly and happily. Mattis turned to Lorica to see her grinning at the rest of them, too.

"Are you—" Mattis almost couldn't believe what he was seeing. "Are you smiling? You don't have any yelling to do about all the feelings that everyone is having right now?"

"Mattis, the mission is accomplished. Once a mission is over, it's time to live. If there's something that binds us, it's this. Emotions. Us. Like Dec said: we're kin now."

Then her smile disappeared quickly. She turned away, but it was too late. Mattis had felt what had sent her smile away; a sliver of a feeling arose inside him that was accompanied by the sensation he now recognized as Lorica's work. She'd had an emotion suddenly that surprised her so much that it jumped into him. That surprised her even more. Mattis felt her feeling that. It was warm. It didn't seem to have the intensity of Mattis's crush on her, but they shared a direction. Lorica's emotion inside Mattis lasted only a second, but it careened around in there and made his heart take a victory lap around his ribcage.

He knew better than to say anything. His silence got him a burst of the sensation of relief directly from Lorica.

A hailing signal rang out.

"Oh, thank Zeltron," Lorica said.

Poe Dameron identified himself and asked to speak to the one in charge. Dec gestured with both hands that Jo should take the comms. Jo stepped forward and threw an arm around Dec's shoulders, and they both laughed.

"Do I hear laughter in there?" Poe demanded sternly. "In a ship that, correct me if I'm wrong, is currently being piloted by a droid, which, correct me if I'm wrong, is against the rules?"

Dec and Jo straightened up. Everyone tensed.

"Because if I'm not wrong, and I tend not to be, and a droid *is* piloting that ship, which is against the rules," Poe continued, "then it seems to me that the rules must be wrong, because that droid is one of the best pilots I've ever seen."

J-Squadron relaxed. Ymmoss laughed fuzzily and rubbed AG's head affectionately. AG was speechless. He wiped his ocular sensor. Jo shot him a little salute. Mattis was amazed. Poe Dameron had seen a lot of pilots.

"Who is talking?" asked Cost. "And where is he?"

Poe requested that AG lead the way back to the base.

"Yes, sir," AG said, setting the coordinates Poe had sent them and signaling Ymmoss to jump.

The stars blurred and stretched around them as J-Squadron returned once again to join the Resistance.

"Will you look at this?" Dec grinned, motioning through the viewscreen. It hadn't been all that long since they'd left D'Qar, but it felt to Mattis like forever. The sight of it made the members of J-Squadron cheer and holler and whoop. They hugged and clapped each other on the backs, and Ymmoss got a terrific scritching.

"Okay, Klimo." Mattis sat back down. "What happened to you back on Vodran? Tell us your story."

Klimo related his tale. He was every bit as excited and unfocused telling the story as he was the day Mattis had met him on the transport to D'Qar. It might have been the same patch of space then and now, heading into the atmosphere of the green orb. Mattis had met Lorica on that transport, too, and had been about to meet the others. Back then, all Mattis wanted was to be a hero of the Resistance, to follow in the footsteps of Skywalker, Organa, and Ackbar.

Now there he was alongside Jerjerrod, Demaris, Hansen, and the rest. He understood that it was far better to fight beside heroes than to be one himself. J-Squadron had won its first battle, or at least survived it. There would surely be more battles to come. Mattis was certain that as long as they stuck together, J-Squadron would win those battles, too.

And someday he'd get to fly an X-wing.

Acker & Blacker wish to thank Michael Siglain
for the opportunity, Jen Heddle for being the
strongest and gentlest of editors, and Annie
Wu for the beautiful, inspiring art. Thanks to
everyone who came on this adventure with us.

BEN ACKER & BEN BLACKER are the creators and writers of the *Thrilling Adventure Hour,* a staged show in the style of old-time radio that is also a contemporary-time podcast. They have written and developed shows for television. They've written comic books. All sorts of comic books including *Star Wars* comic books. Seek them out! They have a short story in a *Star Wars* book called *From a Certain Point of View.* Most recently, at the time of this writing, they've written three books in the Join the Resistance series, including this, the one you're reading right now.

ANNIE WU is an illustrator currently living in Chicago. She is best known for her work in comics, including DC's *Black Canary* and Marvel's *Hawkeye*.